Eight patients later, it was lunchtime, and Lucien was still seething over Dr. Dean Vasquez.

He couldn't get the man out of his head. And Lucien couldn't for the life of him think why. Yes, he was very handsome, and his eyes were a particularly stunning shade of green, but Lucien very rarely found anyone attractive. He barely noticed the way most people looked and almost never got distracted by a handsome face. He usually had to really get to know someone before he could find himself attracted to them. But here he was, unable to get a near stranger out of his head. Or the freckles on Dr. Vasquez's nose, which were so clear, they'd been visible on a screen. Not to mention the dimple that showed in his cheek when he smiled.

It was ridiculous. So what if Dr. Vasquez had looked adorably happy hugging his son? The last thing Lucien needed was to have any kind of feelings for a new colleague.

Dear Reader,

You've picked up my first ever Harlequin Medical Romance, and I'm so thrilled to share Dean and Lucien's story with you!

The Single Dad's Secret is set in a cozy countryside village in leafy Buckinghamshire, just like the village I grew up in, and it gives a fresh twist on the secret child trope.

Dean Vasquez is a hotshot doctor in a busy London practice, whose life is turned upside down when his best friend dies and makes him guardian of her six-year-old son, Rafael. Dean loves Rafael, but he needs help, and there's only one person who can provide it, Rafael's biological father—who has no idea the boy exists.

I loved writing Dean's opposite but perfect match, Dr. Lucien Benedict—a brooding, awkward hero with a heart of gold. And I had so much fun getting to know Dean's son and Lucien's adorable cat (a vital component of any book).

Thank you so much for reading. I hope you enjoy seeing these two characters fall in love as much as I enjoyed writing them.

Love,

Zoey x

THE SINGLE DAD'S SECRET

ZOEY GOMEZ

Recycling programs for this product may not exist in your area.

ISBN-13: 978-1-335-94291-3

The Single Dad's Secret

Harlequin Enterprises ULC
22 Adelaide St. West, 41st Floor
Toronto, Ontario M5H 4E3, Canada
www.Harlequin.com

Printed in U.S.A.

Zoey Gomez lives and writes in sunny Somerset. She saw *Romancing the Stone* at an impressionable age and has dreamed of being a romance writer ever since. She grew up near London, where she studied art and creative writing, and now she sells vintage books and writes novels. A good day is one where she speaks to no one but cats. You can follow @zoeygomezbooks on X and Instagram.

The Single Dad's Secret
is Zoey Gomez's debut title for Harlequin.

Visit the Author Profile page at Harlequin.com.

To Mum. For a lifetime of encouragement, love and support. And, based on all our years of watching *ER* and *Casualty* together, I know you would love this book as much as I do. x

CHAPTER ONE

THIS WAS THE worst Zoom interview of Dean's life. He'd dashed to the kitchen at the last minute, to grab a glass of water, and returned to his desk a moment after the three-person interview panel connected to the meeting. Just in time for them to watch him spill half the water down his arm, and to notice that he was wearing jeans with his suit jacket, because he'd been convinced they wouldn't see him below the waist.

On top of all that, they could probably tell Dean was sitting in his bedroom. He quickly shifted the laptop, so the edge of his unmade bed wasn't in view any more. This was a nightmare. He didn't usually get flustered, but this was no ordinary meeting. The outcome of this interview would affect his entire life.

He took a deep, calming breath, and subtly wiped his wet sleeve on his jeans, as the woman in the centre of the panel introduced herself as Helen, the practice manager. Then a shot of adrenaline rushed through him when she introduced the man on her left as Dr Lucien Benedict. Lucien nodded and said hello as Dean tried to control his surprise.

Lucien's voice was so deep and gravelly Dean swore he felt his own chest vibrate. He didn't look anything like Dean had imagined. His profile on the practice's website had been brief, with no photo. So, as Dean got his first look at Lucien, his gaze ran over the man's features quickly, trying to take him in without being too obvious about it.

Lucien's dark grey eyes were heartbreakingly familiar, but they were paired with sharp cheekbones, a strong jaw and messy, just-got-out-of-bed hair. It was hard to believe he was finally seeing Lucien's face after all these years. It almost felt as if he was seeing a celebrity.

Dean took a sip of water and tried to concentrate on the interview.

'So, first question...' Helen smiled warmly. 'What do you know about our practice?'

Dean smiled back. 'I know it's very different to my current practice, which is located in a pretty chaotic area of South London. But your practice is very similar to the one in which I trained. It's compact, but still busy, with three GPs and a small staff, located in the centre of a small market town with a population of about four thousand people.'

Helen nodded along, smiling, and the last of Dean's nerves disappeared. Things improved further as Dean answered all their questions with ease. He was comfortable talking to people he didn't know, and his charm and bad jokes seemed to be winning two of the interview panel over. Not so much Lucien, who spent most of the interview staring down at his notepad or looking blankly in the general vicinity of the camera, his eyes glazed over, as if he was thinking about something else.

Helen asked her next question. 'Do you predict any challenges in keeping a healthy work-life balance?'

Before Dean could answer, his bedroom door swung open. Dean froze. A six-year-old boy with a shock of messy black hair yawned and stretched his arms above his head.

'Please can you make my breakfast now?'

He stepped closer and punctuated his request by casually lowering one arm and shooting Dean in the head with a suction dart from his plastic gun.

Dean's cheeks flushed as he closed his eyes, sighed, and pulled the dart off his forehead with a pop. Two of the panel laughed kindly, and when Dean's face finally returned to its normal colour he took it as a sign that they would be fun to work with. Lucien, however, simply frowned, and Dean's smile faded. It looked as if Lucien wasn't a fan of kids.

'I guess that answers the work-life balance question!' said Helen.

Dean took Rafael's hand and pulled him on to his knee, hugging him close. 'As you can see, I come with an assistant. So I'll need to balance working with taking care of this monster.' Rafael giggled quietly. 'I'm a single parent,' Dean continued.

It still felt strange to say that. Rafael was the son of his best friend Charlotte, no blood relation to Dean at all. Dean had always been the fun uncle, just like he was everyone's fun friend. He generally avoided responsibility, and had no long-term relationships other than with his job. He'd moved to London for work, and he and Charlotte had all but lost touch. Then, one night about six months ago, he'd got a call to inform him that Charlotte had died in a road traffic accident. And that was when Dean had heard the news that would change his life for ever.

In the event of her death, Charlotte had appointed Dean as Rafael's legal guardian.

That had been one hell of a midnight phone call.

Helen nodded and smiled. 'Accommodation is provided with the GP position. It's been that way here for decades. Where possible, the staff live right by the practice. It's a lovely old brick building, with plenty of room for both of you.'

Lucien looked sharply at Helen, but didn't say anything.

For Dean, an apartment being included in the job was almost too good to be true. It would be a huge relief not to have to search for a place to live on top of moving himself and a kid and starting a new job. That was if he got it.

'We only have one more question,' said Helen, looking down at her notes. 'What draws you to practise medicine here, in Little Champney?'

'That's partly to do with this guy too.' Dean squeezed Rafael's shoulders. 'After he lost his mother, he came to live with me. And, as nice as my flat is, and as professionally fulfilled as I've been working in London, this immediate area isn't somewhere I would ideally want to raise him. We need a new start. Somewhere quieter…a little more child-friendly. Somewhere safe, where we can be part of a community.'

Everything Dean said was true. Especially the part about living in London. He might have some lingering nerves about how he and countryside living would get along, but he'd heard numerous parents discussing incidents of knife crime and drugs outside the local primary school. Enough stories that he couldn't bear the thought of keeping Rafael there.

But there was one other reason he wanted to come to Little Champney, and to their practice in particular. Something he couldn't possibly let anyone know yet. Not even Rafael.

'Well, you'd certainly get that from Little Champney.' Helen put down her pen. 'We know you're a busy man, and we don't want to leave you in suspense. So if you're in agreement, and you could wait for a few moments while we mute the meeting, we can have a discussion and get back to you with a decision right now?'

'Sure, that would be great.'

Dean was surprised, but grateful. If it was bad news he'd rather get it over with as soon as possible.

He waited nervously, his knee bouncing up and down, as Helen muted the meeting. Dean promised to make Rafael some food as soon as the call was over, and with one last plastic dart, this time shot at the mirror, Rafael marched out of the room.

Dean turned back to the screen and his eyes were drawn immediately towards Lucien. Dean took advantage of the fact that the panel wouldn't be able to tell who he was looking at to outright stare at Lucien. The man's lips moved and the other two panellists turned to him. Lucien was talking more now than he had during the whole interview. His eyes flashed when Helen shook her head at him but, try as Dean might, he couldn't lip-read anything they were saying.

A muscle in Lucien's neck flexed as he chewed

on his lower lip, and his thick black hair looked even messier now, as if he'd been running his hands through it. Dean was no expert in body language, but it seemed Lucien might not be his biggest fan.

Dean wasn't sure what he'd expected from Lucien, but it wasn't what he saw on the screen in front of him. With his wide shoulders and thick, muscular arms, barely contained by navy short sleeves, Lucien looked like a Hollywood actor playing a doctor—not a real GP in a country town. Very handsome. Despite the fact that he came across as semi-hostile and monosyllabic.

'Dean?'

Dean snapped out of his reverie.

'We'd love to offer you the position.'

Lucien threw his notebook and pen on to the desk and collapsed into his squeaking office chair. His colleagues had completely ignored his reservations and given Dr Dean Vasquez the job. Outvoted two to one. He was used to them ganging up on him, but that was usually regarding which of the two sandwich places in the town to get lunch from, or whether to get a new coffee machine for the kitchen. He'd erroneously thought they might actually listen to him over something important, like deciding with whom he had to share a workplace and, much more importantly, a house.

Lucien had enjoyed having the house all to

himself for several months. Helen had six kids and a huge mansion near the surgery, so she didn't need a room, and the GP Dr Vasquez would be replacing had been over seventy, quiet as a mouse, and had relocated some time ago, leaving them with locums and some very beautiful antique furniture.

Furniture not compatible with a boisterous child.

Lucien put his head in his hands. He couldn't live with a six-year-old!

Lucien didn't hate children, exactly. He had to deal with them at work almost every day. But he couldn't pretend they didn't make him uncomfortable. He never knew what to say to them—and, to be honest, most children started crying the second they met him. The feeling was mutual.

But he could leave them at work and go home. He worked so hard… He threw everything into being the best doctor he could be. He had no social life and almost no hobbies because being around other people drained him. And being a GP meant interacting with dozens of people every single day. Home was his one relief. The only place he could be alone, relax in peace, and get the recharge he needed in order to cope with the next day of work. And, yes, that might mean he got a little lonely now and again. But who had time for friends when you had as demanding a job as he did?

Dr Vasquez didn't seem the type to understand what Lucien needed. Judging from the interview, he was the polar opposite to Lucien. A chatty, charming extrovert who drew energy from being around lots of people. Lucien, contrary to what other people might think, was happy with his quiet, well-ordered life. Everything was just how he wanted it, at work and at home. He didn't need excitement, chaos or attractive new doctors in his life.

That thought stopped him in his tracks. *Did* he find Dr Vasquez attractive? He shook his head. It was unlikely.

'Stop sulking, Lucien. Dean was by far the best candidate we interviewed, and you know it.'

Helen strode past his desk—where he was not sulking at all, thank you—and patted him on the head.

The panel had interviewed several potential doctors that week, and admittedly none of the others had seemed right to Lucien. But still... He waved her hand away and prepared to meet his first patient.

She turned out to be a woman in her twenties who was sure she was suffering from appendicitis. After a brief examination and a couple of questions, Lucien was able to inform her it was merely trapped wind. Embarrassed, but laughing with relief, she moved forward for a tearful hug. Lucien held out a firm hand for her to shake instead.

It didn't pay to get too familiar with the patients. Before she died, his mother had been Little Champney's GP, and everyone's best friend. She'd given huge swathes of patients her home number and had been available to them at all times.

That stress had made her ill in the end—Lucien was sure of it. A cool, professional distance was what kept him afloat and sane. A safe distance between himself and his patients, and between himself and his fellow doctors. The last time Lucien had got close to someone everything had ended in disaster.

There had been a man once. A man who had put up with his quirks although he hadn't exactly encouraged them. Lucien had succumbed to the constant pressure from his mother to find someone. And that someone had been John. John had been Lucien's neighbour for over a year before Lucien had felt comfortable accepting one of his regular offers of a date. Lucien had been flattered by his attention…maybe he'd convinced himself he could be happy with someone like John. He was well regarded, had a stable job at a local museum… They had interests in common, he was handsome, and Lucien had supposed that might be enough.

He had mistakenly thought John could be someone special, and they'd become so close that

Lucien had allowed himself to be consumed by their relationship. Unfortunately he'd been so preoccupied with it that he'd missed spotting dangerous symptoms in his mother's health. She'd died of a heart attack, which he was sure would have been avoidable if only he'd been paying attention. And evidently Lucien had not been enough for John anyway. He'd left him shortly after Lucien's mother had died.

Never again. He couldn't risk that happening a second time—to a family member or a patient. When it came to Lucien, work was incompatible with a love life. And that was just the way it was.

Eight patients later, it was lunchtime, and Lucien was still seething over Dr Dean Vasquez. He couldn't get the man out of his head.

He couldn't for the life of him think why. Yes, he was very handsome, and his eyes were a particularly stunning shade of green, but Lucien very rarely found anyone attractive. He barely noticed the way most people looked and almost never got distracted by a handsome face. He usually had to really get to know someone before he could find himself attracted to them. But here he was, unable to get a near-stranger out of his head. Or the freckles on Dr Vasquez's nose, which were so clear they'd been visible onscreen. Not to mention the dimple that showed in his cheek when he smiled…

It was ridiculous. So what if Dr Vasquez had

looked adorably happy hugging his son? The last thing Lucien needed was to have any kind of feelings for a new colleague. Especially a likely straight one who had recently lost the mother of his child.

Helen seemed to have some superhuman ability to tell when Lucien was seething, and she approached him at the coffee machine—only to hop back into her defence of their decision to hire Dean, as though there had been no pause in their earlier conversation.

'I know you're not a people person. But Dean seems personable enough for both of you. I bet he'll be super-easy to live with. And being around both him and his son might just help you with that little bedside manner problem you've been having.'

Lucien glared at Helen. He was an exemplary doctor. He'd got the highest marks all through his training, always top of the class. He just happened to have one small blind spot. His bedside manner wasn't all it could be. Especially with children. It had been mentioned in every piece of feedback at medical school and things had never improved. Apparently people found him 'blunt' and 'grumpy'.

But if Helen thought being woken up at five a.m. by a child watching cartoons every morning would fix that she was sorely mistaken.

Lucien downed his coffee and made a second

cup. There was nothing he could do now about Dr Vasquez getting the job. And he certainly couldn't move out of the shared house, so he was stuck with them there too. But the house was big. He could keep his distance from both of them. Dr Vasquez might well be the most extraordinary-looking man Lucien had ever seen, but that didn't change the fact that he was going to make Lucien's life hell if he stuck around.

Besides, Lucien's reservations about giving Dr Vasquez the job weren't entirely selfish. What could an inner-city doctor like him find appealing in a place like Little Champney? He was probably all about bright lights and exciting shifts... crowds and bars and clubs. He'd only applied to work here under some misguided belief that children shouldn't be raised in an urban environment. Soon he'd be bored to tears, realise his mistake, and go running back to the city. And then everyone would be inconvenienced.

Maybe Lucien could save everyone some time and trouble.

He was resolute. He would keep his new houseguests at arm's length and discourage any offers of friendship. Maybe giving them the cold shoulder would help Dr Vasquez realise he'd be better off somewhere else and give Lucien his life back.

With Rafael dropped off for his induction day at Little Champney Primary, Dean headed to the surgery to meet Helen. She would give him the keys to his apartment, and he would unpack the few boxes and bags he'd managed to cram into the back seat and boot of his car. He'd left his furniture and most of his belongings in storage in London. His first day at work wasn't until tomorrow, and maybe after school, when he'd finished unpacking, he and Rafael would have time to take a walk around the town and see what it had to offer.

He drove slowly, wondering if he'd just moved into a storybook. A babbling brook ran all the way through it, parallel to the road. There were green spaces and lush trees everywhere he looked. Colourful flowers grew from pots and troughs along every pavement. People even waved to each other as they strolled along.

He bumped over a cobbled road, creeping past an ancient pub with ivy around the door and a line of little stone cottages with hanging baskets, until he saw an ornate hand-painted sign that read *Doctors' Surgery*, with an arrow pointing to the right.

He'd done some research on Little Champney. It had won Best-Kept Market Town eleven times, it boasted a very exclusive private school on the outskirts of town, and the surrounding acreage seemed to be a top pick among Hollywood actors once they decided to buy a mansion and retire to the sticks.

Dean stood outside the GP practice's reception

door for a full minute, surrounded by an alarming number of terracotta pots bursting with red and yellow tulips. He was breathing as if he'd just run a marathon. This was ridiculous. He'd already met everyone on Zoom. There was no need to feel nervous.

He took a deep breath, regulated his facial expression and pushed the door open.

Lucien was standing right on the other side of it.

'Finally figured out how to use the door, Dr Vasquez?' Lucien asked dryly.

The Zoom call hadn't done Lucien justice. In the flesh, the man was breathtaking. An effect which was strangely intensified by the way he glared at Dean.

Dean suddenly realised he hadn't yet said a word, let alone answered Lucien's question. What had it been again?

He wet his lips and tried to think of something sensible to say. 'Dean!' he exclaimed, embarrassingly. 'Call me Dean.'

A white cat appeared as Dean stepped inside and rubbed against his legs, leaving fur on his black jeans and purring loudly.

He bent down and stroked its soft, warm fur. 'Hello, there.' Dean scratched it behind the ears and its purring intensified. 'Aren't you beautiful?' Dean looked up at Lucien. 'I've never heard of a

GP surgery with a cat before. Libraries and bookshops maybe, but not a surgery.'

'You still haven't,' responded Lucien flatly. 'That's my cat, and she's supposed to be at home.' Lucien frowned down at the cat, then turned his frown on Dean. 'She doesn't like new people. Normally.' Lucien picked up the cat and gently dragged her away from rubbing her face all over Dean's hands. 'Come on, Binxie. Let's get you home.'

Lucien made for the door, glancing back to throw Dean one last disapproving stare. Dean shrugged and walked towards Reception. It wasn't his fault the cat had loved him on sight. He couldn't help feeling rather smug about it. Lucien looked somehow even more intriguing when he was put out.

Helen arrived at Reception with a smile and gestured for him to follow her outside. Dean trotted to keep up with her as she headed straight to his car. He supposed the car park was small enough that she could guess which was his—the fact it was visibly full to bursting with his belongings might have helped too.

'There's a little lane just beside the surgery, almost hidden by weeping willows. Just drive through there and it'll lead you right to the accommodation. I'll meet you there in two minutes!'

The building was just as beautiful as the rest of the town. Red brick, with thick white windowsills, and walls covered in pink climbing roses. It consisted of three floors and held, Dean assumed, three separate flats.

Helen unlocked the front door and ushered him into the ground-floor flat, just as her phone beeped loudly. She grabbed it and read the message.

'Oh, fudge. I have to pop back to the surgery for a minute. Have a look around, and I'll be back to give you the grand tour in a minute!'

With that she was off, and Dean ventured further into the flat alone.

But he wasn't alone for long. Dean stepped into the large flagstone floored kitchen and his hand flew to his chest when he found Lucien crouched over by a double fridge.

'What are you doing in my flat?'

Lucien jumped up and that muscle in his neck twitched again. 'This isn't your flat, Dr Vasquez.'

'No?'

'There aren't any flats—there is one house. And we're sharing it. Apparently.'

'No way.'

A small white blur dashed into the room, and Binxie started eating from the bowl on the floor which Lucien had clearly been filling.

'Yes. Sorry to disappoint.'

'No, I didn't mean— It's fine that you live here.'

'Glad to hear it.'

Dean took a breath. 'Can we start again?'

Lucien waited, giving him nothing, and Dean took that as a sign that the starting again was up to him.

'My name's Dean. I'm your new GP and apparently your new housemate. It's lovely to meet you.'

Lucien looked at Dean's offered hand and then gave it a firm shake. His hand was large and warm, and a thrill ran through Dean as they touched. But by the bored look on Lucien's face he clearly felt absolutely nothing. Which was good. The last thing this situation needed was more complications. Dean was definitely relieved.

'Nice to meet you too,' Lucien murmured.

'So, you and Binxie don't mind two complete strangers moving in?' Dean asked, more as a joke than anything, but by the look on Lucien's face he minded very much.

'I'm sure it will be fine.'

'Rafael's great with animals, so you don't have to worry about him upsetting the cat.'

Lucien nodded wordlessly.

'Well… We'll keep out of your way as much as possible.'

Dean refused to apologise for Rafael's existence, but at the same time he could see how suddenly having a child in the house might be a bit of an adjustment. In fact he knew that better than anyone.

'Helen said she'd be back in a minute, to show me around.'

'Did she get a text from the surgery?'

Dean nodded.

'Then she won't be back for ages—if at all. You'd better come with me.'

Lucien led Dean out of the kitchen and past a living room to a wide staircase. Dean followed Lucien up two flights of stairs, through intermittent splashes of blue, red and yellow light cast by the stained glass windows on the landings. It was a tall house, but each floor wasn't all that big. When they reached the top storey Lucien opened a door. 'This will be your room.'

It was a big space, with arched windows and a sloping ceiling because they were up in the roof. There was a double bed on one side of the room and a single on the other, plus a sofa, desk and a matching wardrobe and dresser.

'I'm glad there's furniture. Did all this belong to the last GP?'

Lucien seemed a little awkward all of a sudden. 'No, this was my room. Dr Haywood couldn't manage all these stairs. I swapped rooms with him after he left.

'Ah. So you're one floor down?'

'Yes. The floor below holds my bedroom and my office. Then the kitchen and living room are on the ground floor. Perhaps—perhaps your son should take my office.'

Dean could tell Lucien had to force that suggestion out. The guy was clearly uncomfortable that they were in the house at all—Dean couldn't sweep his office out from under him as well.

'No, it's fine. Rafael and I can share a room. That's probably more practical anyway.'

Lucien's shoulders visibly relaxed. 'I'll leave you to it, then. I have to get back to work.'

'Thanks for showing me around. By the way, Rafael will probably be here when you finish work…just so you know.'

'Right.'

Lucien looked so sad at the prospect Dean almost felt sorry for him.

Dean started bringing in his and Rafael's belongings from the car. The little courtyard was completely private, and surrounded by tall leafy trees, so he was very brave and left the car boot up between journeys. His city-boy heart was telling him not to, but he was determined to ignore it. He was in the countryside now, and this was how they did things.

He gave the driveway one more furtive look before carrying two boxes and a bag upstairs, walking a lot faster than usual.

Most of the car was taken up with Rafael's toys and books. Dean marvelled at what his life had become. He had a long history of one-night stands and short flings. People often wanted to date him, or go to him for a good time, but they found him very easy to leave. No one ever saw him as a long-term prospect. Since Rafael, he'd found himself utterly uninterested in sex or romance. Right now he had to concentrate on his son. Theirs was the only long-term relationship that mattered.

God, if any of his exes could see him now… They wouldn't recognise him at all. Rafael had changed Dean's life in a heartbeat.

Dean stacked Rafael's books on to the shelf by his bed, and tried to make the room look welcoming and cosy for Rafael's first impression. Dean didn't have much to unpack in the kitchen, aside from a few bits Rafael apparently couldn't live without, Dean's favourite glass mugs and his beloved coffee machine, which had cost close to a month's wages. Lucien didn't seem to have one of his own, so hopefully he wouldn't mind if Dean set it up.

On his last visit to the car, Dean grabbed a few flowers from a plant by the front door that had dozens of blooms to spare. Then he searched the kitchen cupboards for a vase. He left the flowers on the kitchen counter stuffed into a clean bottle from the recycling box with some water inside. Hopefully it would make Rafael smile.

Dean had never even considered having kids. And then, out of the blue, he'd become the one person totally responsible for a small, vulnerable human. As stated in Charlotte's will, his responsibilities were to keep Rafael healthy, make sure he got a good education and give him somewhere safe to live.

Dean had no family to turn to for help—only a brother who was currently in law school and could only provide supposedly encouraging monthly phone calls, earnestly telling Dean he could do anything he put his mind to. And most of the time, Dean was confident he *could* raise Rafael alone. But Rafael deserved more than just him. He deserved as much family in his life as possible. And after a lot of thinking Dean had come to the conclusion that there was only one person who could help with that.

Rafael's biological father.

There had been the small matter of finding him. And then working out if the man was trustworthy. Or even interested. Dean had known he would have to vet him first. Check him out. Make sure he was a good person. Charlotte hadn't talked about Rafael's father much. Dean could only remember her mentioning a first name and a town. And the fact that Rafael had been the result of a casual one-night stand with a fellow medical student at the end of training.

So a few weeks ago Dean had flexed his Google-fu and searched online, not really expecting to find anything. But he'd discovered the man was still exactly where he'd been seven years ago, when Charlotte had last seen him, still doing the same thing. That was a mark in his favour, right?

Dependable, solid, boring… Those were good traits for a father. Dean would have loved a boring dad. Rather than an irresponsible drunk, which was what he'd got.

At that point Dean had almost had second thoughts about the whole endeavour. When Dean was a child, his own mother had let him get attached to several of her partners and he'd lost all of them, which had left him feeling abandoned and unlovable. He wanted something better for Rafael. He couldn't let him get attached to someone who wouldn't stick around. The poor kid had been through enough already. But Dean knew Rafael would have questions one day, and he deserved to have the opportunity to know his biological dad.

After finding the father online, Dean had discovered this surgery's website, and after reading his bio, and trying fruitlessly to tell what kind of man he was from barely thirty words, he'd found a job listing on the site. The practice was looking for a new GP. Dean had already decided he and Rafael needed to start again somewhere new, and this discovery had felt as if the universe was trying to tell him something.

And now here they were.

All of a sudden Dean was about to start living in the same house as the man who had unknowingly fathered Rafael. Lucien had never been told his son existed, and somehow Dean had to keep that a secret until he figured out whether he could trust Lucien with the truth. Whether he could trust Lucien with Rafael's heart.

Exhausted, Dean took a rest on the sofa. It was possibly the softest, comfiest one he'd ever sat on—or maybe he was just the most tired he'd ever been.

From his vantage point he could see the whole living room. There were a few nice pieces of art, but no family photographs. Much of the wall space was taken up by bookshelves. Lucien seemed to be a particular fan of medical textbooks and horror novels. And there was a plethora of healthy-looking pot plants crammed on to the window sill and occasional tables. It was a very homey living room. Dean felt comfortable there already.

Binxie appeared from nowhere and climbed carefully on to Dean's lap. He froze, not wanting to scare her off while she made herself comfortable, kneading his leg with her sharp claws. Dean winced, but didn't move a muscle until she stopped kneading and drifted off to sleep. Binxie's purrs made Dean sleepy and he leaned his head back. The cushions smelled familiar. Where had he smelled that nice clean, woody scent recently? Oh, it smelled like Lucien. That made sense…

He'd come to check Lucien out from afar—or from as far as two colleagues could get in a GP practice. He certainly hadn't expected to be living in Lucien's pocket. Rafael was about to share a house with his biological father. And neither of them knew it. This had the potential to get very complicated, very fast.

It was all up to Lucien, if only he knew it. If Dean found Lucien to be a good, kind man, then Dean would introduce him to his son and let him into Rafael's life. If Dean found him wanting, then he and Rafael would skip town, forget this new life, and no one would ever have to know why they'd come.

CHAPTER TWO

On their first morning sharing a house Dean and Lucien barely saw each other. Dean and Rafael had their own bathroom on the top floor, where Dean showered, then got Rafael ready for school in the familiar morning routine that they had perfected back in London. The only difference was it took a little longer, as Rafael was behaving ten times more chaotically than usual due to his excitement about finally joining Miss Havery's class. He'd taken to her on the induction visit, and apparently she was Rafael's new favourite person.

Dean had decided not to take it personally.

Rafael's footsteps pounded across the landing.

'Walk—don't run!' Dean yelled.

The thought of Rafael toppling down three flights of stairs made his blood run cold for a moment. These semi-irrational fears had started hitting him about ten times a day since Rafael had appeared in his life, and were one of his least favourite parts of suddenly becoming a dad.

By the time Dean made it to the kitchen Rafael had already started looking for the cereal by himself. Half the cupboard doors were open, but he'd finally located the right one—judging from the four boxes of cereal stacked haphazardly on the kitchen floor.

Dean picked up Rafael's favourite and put the rest away. 'Climb up on the stool and I'll pour you a bowl.'

Rafael placed his packed school bag by the front door and then started putting his shoes on.

'Don't get ahead of yourself, buddy. We're not ready for shoes yet.'

Dean busied himself pouring Frosty Stars into Rafael's favourite yellow bowl. He got out the milk, and dropped some bread into the toaster for himself. He barely noticed Lucien come into the room, his mind occupied with all the tasks they had to complete before he could walk Rafael to school.

'Careful!' Lucien shouted, and Dean whipped around.

Rafael held a huge four-pint milk carton awkwardly in his tiny arms, while a large pool of milk spread over the counter and dripped on to the floor. Binxie appeared out of nowhere to help clean up the milk on the floor, and Rafael giggled.

'Oh, God.' Dean grabbed the carton out of Rafael's hands and reached for a cloth. 'Not really a laughing matter, Raf. You knew that was too big for you.'

'I did not!'

'Cats aren't supposed to drink cow's milk,' Lucien muttered.

That was news to Dean.

'They're lactose intolerant,' Lucien continued.

He picked up Binxie with one hand and deposited her by her bowl of water in the corner.

Dean spent a couple of minutes wiping up all the milk and wringing out the cloth into the sink. The room was silent, but Dean could see Lucien out of the corner of his eye, sitting as far away from Rafael as possible and eating toast and coffee while reading a medical journal. Rafael hadn't eaten a bite. He sat, legs dangling off the stool, one shoe on and one shoe off, staring at the bowl.

'Eat up! We don't have long before we have to leave.'

'I don't want it.'

'You have to eat breakfast. It'll keep you strong all day.'

'Don't want to.'

'You wanted cereal two minutes ago.'

Rafael stared at the bowl. 'It's too milky.'

'And why's that?'

'It was an accident!' Rafael shouted.

Lucien glared at them over the top of his medical journal.

Rafael was usually so good and quiet in the

mornings. This was not making the first impression on Lucien that Dean would have liked.

'I know it was an accident, Raf. We all have them. How about you eat my toast instead?'

Rafael crossed his arms and glared at the table. 'I'm not going to school, so I don't need toast.'

Dean heaved a sigh. Where was this suddenly coming from?

He sat down on the stool next to Rafael and talked to him quietly and calmly. 'I know you're probably a bit overwhelmed with all the new things going on today, but I could really use your help. I need you to eat one piece of toast before you can leave the table.'

'No!' Rafael shouted, and kicked out in frustration.

Unfortunately he hit Dean with the foot wearing a shoe.

Dean cursed under his breath and jumped up, rubbing his shin furiously. Rafael looked just as shocked as Dean felt.

Lucien rose from his chair in the corner, grabbed his stuff and strode towards the front door without a word, half a slice of toast still gripped between his teeth.

'Sorry, Dean! I didn't mean to get you.' Rafael's eyes were big and watery.

'I know, buddy. It's okay, it didn't hurt,' Dean lied.

The kid had a hell of a left foot on him.

The front door slammed and Dean sighed. Lucien leaving in disgust at the first sign of a little morning chaos wasn't the best sign. But Dean couldn't worry about that now.

He wiped Rafael's face gently with the soft sleeve of his sweater until his tears were all gone. 'Are you nervous about your new school? Is that why you're all out of sorts?'

Rafael turned his big grey eyes up at Dean and gazed at him for a moment. 'You're meant to use a tissue, not your sleeve.' he said, parroting back Dean's oft-used admonishment to Rafael.

'That's for your nose. Tears are okay—they're only water.' Dean squeezed Rafael's shoulder.

'I'm not nervous. I just want to stay with you.'

'You'll have much more fun at school than you would with me. And I'll see you right after. You'll forget all about me once you start having fun.' Dean smoothed Rafael's hair back into place.

'I miss Mummy.'

It felt as if a bucket of ice-cold water had been thrown over Dean's head.

'Of course you do, sweetheart.'

Dean took a deep breath as Rafael flung his arms around Dean's neck. He wrapped the boy in a hug and tried to think of something that would cheer Rafael up.

'It's your birthday next week. Think of all the cake and presents you're going to get.'

You probably weren't supposed to cheer children up with material things, but by God Dean was planning to buy him a lot of presents.

'Mummy won't be here.'

And that was Dean done for.

He wiped his own eyes on his sleeve, sniffed, and took a steadying breath.

'I miss her too.' He pulled back and caught Rafael's gaze. 'I'm sorry, but I'm all you've got now. You're all I've got, too. It's just you and me, Raf. And I promise that we're going to be fine.'

Rafael gave him a watery smile and Dean exhaled, relieved that he seemed to be cheering up. He smiled conspiratorially at Rafael. 'I don't think we've made a very good first impression on Lucien.'

'I like him,' answered Rafael.

'Same here.'

Dean just hoped he could like them too.

'Can I have your toast now?'

Dean laughed and handed it over.

Finally at the practice, after dropping Rafael at school, Dean checked the time. He still had ten minutes free before eight-thirty, so he pulled out his phone and started filming a video.

'Hi, everyone. Dr Dean here. I promised to show you my brand-spanking-new practice, so here it is.' He switched to main camera and stepped through the practice entrance. 'I won't say where it is, because I don't want any of you lot stalking me, but we have gone through the looking glass, guys. We are not in London any more. Imagine the opposite of London and that's where we are. Thatched roofs, roses around every door, fields full of buttercups—all that good stuff.'

He walked through the empty reception area and waiting room. Helen greeted him from the break room and he panned left to leave her out of the video.

'Morning! You want to be on Instagram live?'

'Sure, why not?'

She laughed and waved at the camera as he pointed it at her. 'This is my wonderful new boss…'

'Oh, I'm hardly your boss.'

'But you *are* wonderful?'

'Of course!'

He spoke from behind the camera a little more as he continued through the corridors. The place was bigger than he remembered it being. When he arrived at his consulting room he was pleased to find that someone had already put a sign on his door reading *Dr Vasquez*. He made sure to get a good shot of that on the video, then opened the door.

Only to find Lucien inside.

'Oh, hey.' Dean twisted his hand so that the camera pointed to his desk instead. 'Sorry guys, tour's over. I have to get to work now.'

'What on earth are you doing?' asked Lucien.

'Shouldn't I be the one asking you that?'

Lucien frowned, as if confused, and Dean looked back over his shoulder to check that his name was indeed on the door, as he'd thought.

'I was just getting some latex gloves,' said Lucien as he turned away to shuffle some boxes around on the shelf. 'You have three spare boxes in here for some reason.'

'It's fine,' said Dean, with a smile. 'You're welcome in my consulting room any time.'

Dean shoved his phone in his pocket.

'Why do you make everything sound suggestive?' Lucien mumbled.

Dean hadn't meant to, but he was glad to hear that Lucien thought so. He hesitated. Should he take this opportunity to apologise for Rafael's difficult morning? It might be best not to bring it up. After all, Rafael hadn't really done anything wrong. He'd been understandably upset and nervous. Dean's shin was the only real victim.

'I was just updating my Instagram,' Dean said in answer to Lucien's initial question.

'Who were you talking to?'

'My followers.'

Lucien rolled his eyes. 'Who on earth would be interested in seeing this?'

'Over a million people say they find my content pretty interesting.'

'*How* many?' Lucien gaped at him.

Dean grinned. 'I have one point two million followers.'

'How?' Lucien sounded absolutely gobsmacked.

'I'll try not to take offence at your tone, Dr Benedict,' Dean joked. 'I use my account to educate people about what GPs do. There's a lot of misinformation out there. I like to present a "warts and all" view of the reality.'

'Well, I hope you don't include anyone's personal information.'

'Of course not. I'm completely discreet.'

'And I hope I wasn't in that video. I didn't give my permission for you to film me.'

'It's fine. I missed you out.'

Dean hoped he had—he'd already posted the video. He'd check it in a minute.

'Be more careful in future. There's a reason I don't bother with all that social media nonsense. I have no interest in being put online.'

'Oh, that's right...you don't even have a picture on your profile.'

'What?'

'On the practice website. Your profile is just a bio.'

Lucien's cheeks coloured a bit and he picked up his box of gloves. 'I'm a very private person.'

'Nothing wrong with that.'

Lucien grunted and left, saying, 'You should be working—not filming.'

Dean soon forgot all about the video when

he sat down to run through some of the admin already piled up on his desk, and to check his schedule for the day. He signed in to his computer and tried to find his way around the system. It was almost the same as the one they'd used at his last practice. Just a few slight differences.

What were his old colleagues back in London doing now? he wondered. With any luck it wouldn't be long before his new colleagues here became his friends, but that didn't stop him missing his old ones. They'd all worked hard at the London practice, but they'd still made the effort to socialise when they could—even if it was just going for a wind-down drink on a Friday evening when they were all exhausted from a week at work.

Around this time of year was normally when his old practice started doing their educational school visits, teaching kids first aid and telling them what to do in an emergency. He loved meeting new people, and those visits always fulfilled that tiny part of him that had always secretly wanted to perform in front of an audience. Or maybe his ego just liked him being the centre of attention now and again. Hence his Instagram account, he supposed.

He fought off a wave of homesickness. He'd have to make sure to find time later on to text his old friends and see how they were doing without him.

Dean welcomed the first patient of his morning surgery into his consulting room at ten past nine. It felt somehow momentous, his first ever patient here, but he decided not to say anything. No need to make it weird.

He looped his pink stethoscope around his neck and sat down at his desk, twisting the chair to face his patient, who was a man of around fifty, wearing jeans and a plaid jacket caked in mud.

'What can I help you with today?'

'You the new one, then?' his patient asked.

Dean grinned. 'I am. And you're my first ever patient.'

'Ever? I didn't volunteer to be anyone's guinea pig.'

'Sorry, I meant my first one here,' Dean explained. 'I've been a GP elsewhere for several years.'

And now he'd made it weird.

'I'm only joking, son. I don't mind being a guinea pig—everyone's got to start somewhere.'

'Quite right. So, what brings you in today?'

'My stomach's giving me a heck of a problem.'

'In what way?'

'It hurts when I move. I can't stand up without feeling like I'm being stabbed.'

'Have you experienced any nausea or problems eating?'

'No, Doc.'

Dean took a full history of the patient's symptoms, then pushed his chair back. 'Okay, if you'd like to lie on your back on the examination table and pull up your shirt, I'll take a quick look.'

The patient lay back, getting mud from his jeans all over the white paper cover, and groaned as he pulled his muddy boots on to the foot of the bed. He yanked up his T-shirt to reveal a large red patch of skin, turning blue in the centre.

'That's a nasty bruise,' said Dean. 'Any idea what caused that?'

'Not sure, Doc. Although, now you ask, the pains did start after Maisy kicked me in the stomach.'

'Who's that?' Dean frowned. 'Your wife? Or—'

'My cow.'

Dean drew back. 'Your cow?'

'She was about to drop a calf and I tried to check how far along she was. She rather took against it.'

'Oh, you were trying to…?' Dean gestured with one arm.

Using his very limited knowledge of what farmers did to help cows give birth, he wasn't surprised she'd kicked him. Dean had been kicked himself doing much less invasive procedures during a patient's childbirth. His current patient nodded, wincing as Dean used both hands to gently press over the area. He didn't think any ribs had been fractured, but he couldn't be sure.

'I think we might have to get you an X-ray.

Make sure she hasn't knocked anything out of whack.'

'Very technical, Doc.'

'I do try.'

Dean wrote up the patient's notes and ordered the X-ray, then whistled happily as he cleaned the mud off the examination table. He thought he'd seen everything back in London, but he was thrilled to learn there were still new experiences to be had in his new practice.

'Someone's happy.' Helen knocked briskly on the door as she opened it, and sniffed the air suspiciously. 'Which is unusual in a room that smells like manure.'

'Yeah, I think I might need a bucket and a mop rather than antiseptic wipes.'

'Well, it will have to wait. I've got a patient on the line for you.'

She pointed at the phone on Dean's desk. He dropped the wipes in the wastebasket and sat down on his chair, picking up the phone and just managing to press the right button as he spun from the momentum.

'This is Dr Vasquez. How can I help?'

He was met with the heavy breath of someone in a panic. 'I wanted Dr Benedict, but they said he's busy.'

'I'm sure I can help you. Tell me what you need.'

'My wife's pregnant, but she's not due for another week. I think she's having it now. What do I do? Her contractions are only six minutes apart!'

Trying to assess the situation, Dean asked a simple question. 'Is this her first child?'

'No, you idiot, this is her husband.'

Dean tried to hold in a laugh. 'I'm sorry, I wasn't clear. Is this your wife's first pregnancy?'

'Yes.'

'Okay. Keep calm…everything's going to be fine.' Dean heard someone groaning in the background. 'How's she doing?'

The man mumbled something away from the phone. 'I asked her, but she swore at me. A lot.'

Dean smiled. If he was going through labour he'd be swearing too. At the very least. 'What's in your birth plan? Is it a home birth or in the hospital?

The man's breathing calmed slowly. 'Hospital. I was supposed to drive us, but my car is at the garage. I thought I had another week… I've called an ambulance.'

'Okay, that's wonderful.'

'But what if the baby comes now? I need someone on the line to help me. Dr Benedict told me to call him if I was worried about anything. Well, I'm worried.'

Dean's door swung open and Lucien stood there, looking handsomely dishevelled.

'Speak of the devil.' Dean gestured questioningly between Lucien and the phone and Lucien nodded, holding his hand out for the receiver. 'Dr Benedict's just arrived—I'm passing you over.'

Lucien leaned against Dean's desk and Dean sat back in his chair, looking at his computer monitor but listening to Lucien's side of the conversation.

'Six minutes? The ambulance should have plenty of time to get to the hospital. There's really no need to panic.'

Dean could smell Lucien's woodsy scent again. Was it his aftershave or his shampoo? It was intoxicating… Dean tried not to take in any obvious deep breaths. Lucien's hip was only an inch away from Dean's arm, and Dean could feel the man's body heat. Lucien shifted as he answered a question and his hip pushed against Dean's elbow. Lucien was staring out of the window as he spoke, not paying Dean any attention at all. He probably thought he was pressed against Dean's chair.

Dean held his breath and didn't move a muscle. His elbow tingled where it was pressed against Lucien's warm, solid form. He hadn't felt this ridiculously affected by something since he was a teenager.

Lucien talked calmly to the patient for a few more minutes, until the ambulance arrived, then said his goodbyes and handed Dean back the phone, finally pulling away from his arm. Dean saw Lucien look down at their point of contact in surprise. So he really hadn't known it was happening.

Dean smiled and spoke quickly. 'Things are very different here.'

'What do you mean?' asked Lucien.

'I've never heard of a patient calling their GP for help during childbirth. They usually contact their midwife or the hospital.'

'He's my grandmother's gardener. He's been very nervous about things all through the pregnancy. I've been trying to help.'

That was very sweet. And it went above and beyond Lucien's job description. Maybe he wasn't as closed off as he seemed.

During a short lull between patients, Dean stepped into the break room to grab a drink.

'Helen! Just the person I wanted to see.'

'This sounds ominous. What do you need?' Helen looked up from her tea.

'Do we do any school visits? You know…teaching the kids basic CPR or first aid?'

'As it happens, I've organised for Lucien to do something just like that next week.' She paused. 'I haven't told him yet…'

'Great! It worked really well at my last practice. We visited workplaces too. The more people who know CPR the better.'

'Absolutely. You should join him—it would be

the perfect opportunity for you to get to know your new community.'

Lucien appeared from his consulting room and Dean smiled. 'You up for that, Lucien?'

'Sorry, what?'

Lucien looked confused and sleepy, which seemed to be his default expression. Admittedly, it wasn't an unattractive one.

'You and I are going to find some spare time and impart wisdom and confidence to the kids of the local community.'

What could be a better test for someone's dad potential than seeing him interact with a classroom full of kids?

'Spare time? What's that?' Lucien asked grumpily. He narrowed his eyes at Dean. 'Are you just trying to find endearing things to put on Instagram and gain you more followers?'

Dean tutted. 'No. You can't film strangers' kids and put them online. Not everything I do is for content. Sometimes I actually do wonderful, selfless things out of the goodness of my own heart.'

Helen chuckled. 'Come on, Lucien,' she encouraged. 'This'll be good for you. And it'd help you with you know what,' she said more quietly.

What the heck was 'you know what'? Dean wondered.

'It'll be fun. I promise.' Dean did his best to give Lucien the puppy-eyed look that he was reliably informed was irresistible.

Lucien just raised an eyebrow and looked at him in silence, reminding Dean of every disapproving teacher he'd ever had.

'Fine,' said Lucien, turning on his heel and disappearing back into his room.

Dean smiled. He knew he still had it.

At lunchtime, Lucien made himself a coffee in the break room and leaned against the counter drinking it. The mug warmed his hands, and the delicious scent calmed his nerves. Dean and Helen sat at the table on the other side of the room, eating. Lucien was reluctant to join them in case they roped him into something else ridiculous.

This morning at home had been tense. Lucien didn't know much about children, but even he'd been able to surmise that the child might be having trouble settling into his new environment. So he had decided to leave, in case his presence was making things worse. Dean looked much happier now, so Lucien hoped the child had cheered up once he'd made himself scarce.

Nice to know his terrible success rate with kids had not improved one iota. If he was in the room, kids cried.

He'd heard Rafael call Dean by his name, just before the door had shut behind him. Not Daddy—just Dean. Not that it was any of Lucien's business, but he couldn't help but ponder over it. Perhaps the child had lived with his mother and hadn't seen Dean very much…or maybe he'd called someone else Daddy.

Lucien sat down and pulled out his phone. The only apps he had were news sites and medical databases. Did you have to join Instagram to look up someone's account?

His eyes met Dean's across the room and Lucien shoved his phone back in his pocket.

Even eating, Dean looked attractive. It was unfair. Dean's gaze slid to Lucien again, even as he chatted with Helen, and a hot flush ran through Lucien's body. Lucien studiously avoided making eye contact again, unwilling to feel so thoroughly undone at work, and he soon zoned out, sipping his coffee and thinking about a patient.

'What's on your mind?'

Lucien jumped. He hadn't known Dean was still in the room, let alone paying him any attention. 'Why should anything be on my mind?'

'You've been glaring at that window for five minutes straight. What did it do to you?'

'It's nothing. I'm just contemplating a patient.'

Dean slid on to the seat beside him. 'Tell me.'

Lucien sighed. If Dean must insist on pressing his warm body up against him, and smelling so distractingly good, he could hardly be blamed for doing exactly as the man asked.

'I haven't seen her in the consulting room for quite some time, but she used to suffer badly from auditory and visual hallucinations. I prescribed her antipsychotic meds and CBT. And she hasn't been back in since.'

'That's promising,' said Dean.

'I hoped so. But an aunt of hers cornered me in the shop yesterday. She thinks the patient's mental health may have recently declined.'

'That's not good,' said Dean. 'So what are you going to do?'

'What can I do? I'll wait for her to make an appointment. And if she does, I'll provide her with the appropriate treatment.'

'Is that it?'

'What would you have me do? Visit her at home out of the blue and ask how she is?'

Which, he realised as he said it, was exactly what his mother would have done.

Back when Lucien's mother had been the village GP her door was never closed. She'd pick up a call from a patient day or night. Even if it meant being pulled away from Lucien's bedtime story, or missing his big line in a school play. And her endless, ceaseless generosity had killed her in the end. Run her into the ground. She'd never had a day off in her life.

Lucien never wanted to be like that. When he closed the door to his home, it was closed. That didn't mean he wouldn't do whatever it took to care for his patients. But he never crossed that line into taking his emotions home or getting personally involved.

'That would be inappropriate,' he said. 'I suggested that her aunt encourage her to make an appointment with me if she feels she needs help. That's all I can do.'

'We need a doctor out here!'

The desperate shout from outside broke the calm. Dean dropped his sandwich and jumped up to look out of the open window.

'We're on our way!' Dean called out of the window, then turned back. 'Someone's collapsed in the car park. Looks to be a male in his sixties.'

Dean and Lucien ran outside to find a man on the ground. His head had only missed the kerb by inches, and most of his body was crammed into the small space between two cars.

A woman stood over him. 'Look at all the commotion you've caused, Harold.'

'No commotion. It's what we're here for,' Dean reassured her smoothly.

Lucien knelt awkwardly by the man's shoulders, unable to get any closer, and felt for a pulse in his neck. 'Can you hear me, sir?'

Harold groaned.

'My husband does have an appointment, but we're a bit early.'

'It's okay. We won't make you wait until the allotted time,' said Dean.

Typical Dean, thought Lucien, joking at this of all times.

'What was he coming in for? Do you know?' he asked Harold's wife.

'Oh, he's been having terrible headaches. He refused to make an appointment, but today he couldn't see for a few seconds. I should have made him come in sooner.'

'Don't worry,' said Dean.

'I don't like his pulse,' said Lucien. 'Let's get him inside and call an ambulance.'

Dean nodded and called to Helen, who was watching from the doorway. 'We need the stretcher, and an ambulance here as soon as possible.' He turned back to Harold's wife. 'Just a precaution.'

'Whose are these cars?' shouted Lucien. 'We need to get at least one moved.'

Helen ran inside. She returned quickly carrying the lightweight stretcher, a blanket and a resuscitation kit. 'The ambulance should arrive in ten. I've checked inside and the cars don't belong to anyone here.'

Thoughtless shoppers were always parking their cars in the practice's small car park. Not only was it a pain, it was also technically illegal. This time Lucien was going to take their number plates and damn well report them to the police.

Dean situated the stretcher as close as possible to the man on the pavement, then he and Lucien got into position to transfer their patient. But Harold's face was dangerously pale, so before they moved him Lucien checked his pulse again. He couldn't find one.

'Damn, I've lost the pulse.'

Lucien gently tipped Harold's head back, then leaned his head down close to his face to check for breath. Nothing. Lucien felt the carotid artery with his fingers, but still couldn't find a pulse. He was going to have to try CPR in this ridiculously enclosed space.

He stood, swung his leg over the man's body and straddled him, then started compressions on the patient's chest using both hands. 'Dr Vasquez,' he barked. 'I need your help. Sit by his head.'

Dean jumped to follow his instructions, and they took it in turns, Lucien compressing, then giving his aching shoulders a welcome rest for a few seconds while Dean squeezed the bag valve mask Helen had brought out with the stretcher. They worked together in perfect unison, keeping Harold alive until the ambulance siren indicated that help was almost there.

When the paramedics reached them, Lucien climbed off the patient and jumped out of their way, letting them work. The paramedics, more practised in manoeuvring patients out of tricky places, got Harold on to a stretcher in seconds and continued to perform CPR as they swept him off to the ambulance.

Adrenaline rushed through Lucien's entire body, and he breathed hard as he shook out his burning muscles. He wiped his sweaty forehead on the bottom of his shirt, unwittingly flashing his stomach to all and sundry in the process. He noticed Dean staring and tucked his shirt back in carefully, embarrassed.

Dean was helping the patient's wife over to the back of the ambulance, one arm around her shoulders, talking to her quietly. He held her hand as she climbed the steps, and gently shut the door behind her.

Everything seemed very quiet after all the excitement. Luckily it was a slow afternoon and there wasn't a waiting room full of patients clamouring to be seen. Dr Vasquez insisted on taking the only waiting patient, and Lucien downed an entire bottle of water, then took the opportunity to talk to Helen while Dean was out of the way.

'Helen? Do you have Instagram?'

'Yes?'

'I suppose Dr Vasquez has convinced you to follow him already?'

'As a matter of fact, I followed him a while ago—just after his interview.'

Lucien nodded, not sure how to ask what he wanted to ask.

'Do you want his handle so you can follow him?'

'God, no. But…' Lucien paused. 'He was filming inside the practice earlier. I would like to check if he was being suitably discreet. Medical records. Privacy. All that.'

'Wouldn't it be easier to just talk to him?'

'If you don't want to help me, that's absolutely fine.'

'Of course I do. Here.' Helen held out her phone, already open to Dean's profile, and Lucien took it.

The newest post was a video.

'Have you watched this yet?' Lucien asked.

'Hmm?' Helen was already captivated by whatever work she was doing on her computer screen.

'Never mind. Thank you.' Lucien moved across the room to the window and pressed play on the video.

It began outside the surgery, focused on Dean's face, his eyes squinting shut against the morning sunlight, which flashed off his bright green eyes when he blinked. He rubbed a hand quickly through his hair, perhaps to tidy it for the camera. With the birds chirping happily in the background it sounded idyllic.

'Hi, everyone…'

His voice sounded deeper on the recording.

'I promised to show you my brand-spanking-new practice, so here it is.'

He smiled shyly at the camera, and Lucien spotted the dimple in his cheek. He could practically hear Dean's followers sighing in adoration.

Dean switched the view from front-facing to back and continued into the practice. He didn't show any of the signage or posters outside that viewers might use to identify the location, which was smart, Lucien grudgingly admitted. Dean made a joke about avoiding stalkers and Lucien couldn't help but smile. After he'd entered the practice and greeted Helen, he continued alone through the corridor.

The background noise receded and Dean talked quietly. It suddenly felt more intimate, like one of those ASMR videos Helen watched to help her meditate at lunchtimes. Dean's deep, gentle tones sent a little shiver down Lucien's spine. He was starting to understand how Dean might have amassed a million followers.

Lucien glanced over at Helen, but she was still ignoring him. He moved slightly, so he was hidden by the break room fridge, then carried on watching.

'I'm a little bit nervous, actually,' Dean was saying. 'It's always scary starting somewhere new, trying to fit in with a group of people who've known each other for years.'

It hadn't occurred to Lucien that Dean would be nervous. Or that he was even capable of the emotion. He seemed so confident and laid-back about everything.

'Hopefully I won't annoy them too much. I know exactly how annoying I can be from all of your comments,' he said, the smile audible in his voice. 'Oh, I got myself a new stethoscope to celebrate the move.' Dean flashed the end of a hot pink stethoscope in front of the camera. 'They all seem really nice so far. Especially my fellow GP. He's pretty cool.'

Lucien's heart stuttered. He was stunned to be mentioned.

'Oh, hey, here's my room.'

The camera zoomed in on Dean's nameplate. Dean swung his door open wide, and Lucien flinched as he saw his own back on the video. He'd almost forgotten why he was watching it in the first place. He saw himself turn around, holding the box of latex gloves like an idiot.

He could see the moment Dean thought he'd turned the camera away, but he hadn't turned it far enough, and Lucien remained clearly visible on the far right-hand side of the shot. Was that really what his hair looked like? He looked as if he'd been freshly dragged through a field. Lucien didn't normally worry about his appearance, but he didn't like to look sloppy. What on earth had he been doing to look so dishevelled?

On the video, after Lucien had asked Dean what he was doing, and Dean had turned to look at the name on the door, the camera stayed on Lucien and showed him very clearly looking Dean up and down, blatantly checking him out before he could turn back around.

Lucien cursed under his breath. Unable to find any way of rewinding the video only a little way, he impatiently watched the whole thing again, his heart racing until he got to the part he really wanted to rewatch. It was impossible to miss. His eyes swept over Dean's body from top to bottom then up again. On the screen Dean said something else, and ended the video, but Lucien wasn't paying much attention.

His cheeks were hot with embarrassment. Up to a million random strangers would now have seen him clearly checking Dean out. He didn't even remember doing it—it must have been instinctual. But it was so obvious. No one would miss it. Dean must have seen it too. And Helen. Everyone would think he was interested in Dean. And he most certainly was not.

Lucien closed down everything on Helen's phone and leaned his forehead heavily on the fridge. This was exactly why he hated social media.

He handed Helen back her phone and ignored her curious look. If Dean hadn't been so careless this would never have happened. Maybe he'd done it on purpose? A boost for his ego and a laugh for his fans all in one?

Lucien stormed through the open door of Dean's consulting room to find him sitting on the edge of his desk, texting and laughing to himself. He looked up and smiled.

'Talking to your adoring fans again?' Lucien asked scathingly.

Dean didn't seem to notice his tone and smiled warmly. 'No. I'm still part of my old practice's WhatsApp group and they're asking me what we did today. They're getting a real kick out of all the crazy countryside shenanigans.'

Lucien could just imagine what that conversation was like. Dean telling his sophisticated city friends about the country bumpkins.

'Well, I don't know what cases you were used to in London. Shootings and terminal rudeness, I don't doubt. But the patients here are just as important and deserving of respect.'

'Oh, no, I wasn't—'

'And I thought I asked you not to put me online. I suppose you thought it would be funny to just do it anyway?'

Dean frowned, looking genuinely confused. Then his expression changed to one of horror and he started tapping away on his phone. 'Oh, God, I forgot to check the video. Were you on there? I really thought I'd moved the camera away.'

Dean paused as he watched the video he'd posted earlier—evidently for the first time, unless he was a skilled actor on top of all his other annoying talents.

Dean swore quietly. 'I'm so sorry. I never would have done that on purpose. I know I didn't have your permission. I'll delete it.'

Lucien's shoulders dropped, his anger deflated. Dean clearly hadn't done it on purpose. After all, it wasn't his fault Lucien found him physically attractive and was stupid enough to have checked him out on camera. Part of him wanted to tell Dean not to delete it—it had been a nice video aside from Lucien's bit part ruining it. But at the same time he couldn't bear his secret attraction being up there for eternity for all to see.

Unless… Maybe it wasn't obvious to anyone else? Maybe he was just being paranoid?

'Were you checking me out?' Dean was staring at his phone.

Lucien stopped dead, closed his eyes and pinched the top of his nose. 'This is mortifying.'

Maybe if he left now he could pretend none of this had ever happened.

Dean chuckled softly. 'I'm gonna delete it… it's okay.'

Lucien forced himself to make eye contact, then watched as Dean's gaze returned to his phone and ran across his screen for a moment.

'You didn't read any of the comments, did you?' Dean asked.

'No. Why?'

'No reason.'

Oh, this couldn't be good.

Lucien crossed the room and leaned closer to Dean, trying to get a look at the comments.

I assume that's the other GP you mentioned? The one you like? I can see why!

Hashtag hot doctors! Is everyone who works there gorgeous?

Oh, my God, the sexual tension. I can see the fanfic being written as we speak!

'Fanfic?' said Lucien.

'Don't ask.' Dean scrolled some more.

'I can't believe how many comments there are,' said Lucien, watching as hundreds of comments flashed across the screen.

'Yeah, and they're mostly about you.'

Lucien decided to ignore that. 'Do you always get this many?'

Dean shrugged. 'I always get interaction for videos.' He paused. 'Have you finished reading? I'm gonna delete it now.'

'Can you delete something even after it gets...' Lucien checked the number by the heart symbol '...forty-two thousand hearts?'

Dean smiled. 'They're called "likes". But I like hearts better. And, sure, you can delete stuff any time you want.'

Lucien suddenly felt a small and ridiculous sense of loss at the thought of the one video of them together being erased.

He shook his head to force the thought away. 'I'm finished reading.'

But Dean must have sensed something, because he looked searchingly up at Lucien for a moment.

Being in such close proximity to Dean's green eyes was quite breathtaking, and Lucien's pulse quickened. He swallowed dryly.

'I can archive it,' said Dean. 'That will make it invisible to the public, but it will still be there.'

Lucien found himself nodding. 'Yes. Do that.'

CHAPTER THREE

LUCIEN SIGHED HEAVILY and shifted in his uncomfortable chair. Helen had been organising furiously behind the scenes and had arranged their first visit to the local primary school. Lucien had experienced easier mornings. Like the home visit during which he had treated a family of eight suffering from gastroesophageal reflux disease and uncontrollable projectile vomiting. He had enough trouble getting along with one child, and now he found himself sitting in a school filled with the little creatures.

He and Dean were perched on plastic chairs at the front of the hall, between a piano and an inexplicably large papier-mâché palm tree. The children all sat in rows on a shiny wooden floor marked out for various games, their legs crossed and their fingers on their lips after their teacher had ordered it.

Rafael waved excitedly at Lucien from the third row, and Lucien couldn't help but smile back. He glanced over at Dean, who he was surprised to find was already looking at him.

The teacher introduced them as Dr Dean and Dr Lucien with what seemed like unnecessarily enthusiastic vigour, as though they were famous rock stars rather than just local GPs. But the kids ate it up and let out an excited noise en masse. To be fair, Dean didn't look completely unlike a rock star. He jumped up and greeted the kids in the same manner as the teacher, but on him the enthusiasm seemed authentic. Dean explained to the children what he and Lucien were there to do, and made some jokes, and by the time he'd finished talking the kids were practically vibrating with excitement.

How did he do that?

Dean came over and stood near Lucien, before continuing to talk to the children. 'Accidents happen, and at some point everyone gets a little bit hurt. It's never fun, but we can help it feel better by acting quickly and calmly to help! That's called first aid. Has anyone heard of that before?'

A chorus of several dozen kids chanted, 'Yes, Dr Dean!' and Lucien smiled to himself.

He hadn't set foot in a school since he was small enough to fit into one of those tiny chairs. But not much had changed. The faint smell of school dinners and the walls covered with children's paintings and alphabet charts were giving him a serious nostalgia rush. And he was rather enjoying it. He supposed you missed out on this kind of thing when you didn't have kids…

'If someone gets hurt or feels ill,' Dean continued, 'there are a few simple things to remember. First, try to find a trusted adult and get help, and then, if you can't find one, always call 999. Then you'll get someone a bit like me to come and help you.'

A little girl put her hand up.

'Yes?'

'If I call 999, will you answer?'

Dean laughed kindly. 'Sadly not. But you'll always find someone very nice and helpful on the other end. Okay—second thing: only help if it's safe for you to do so. Keep yourself safe first.'

Lucien saw a few confused faces, and it seemed that Dean noticed the same.

'That means,' Dean continued, 'if someone gets into trouble in a pond, don't jump in to help. That would just make two people in trouble instead of one.'

There were a few nods.

Dean walked back and forth across the hall in front of the kids as he spoke, making eye contact with them. They all watched him, enraptured.

'Okay, what are some common injuries that you can think of? Hands up.'

Twenty kids' hands shot up at once, some children wriggling in place desperately. Dean laughed and pointed at the kids one by one until they'd all had a go. Some suggestions were sensible, like cuts, burns and nose bleeds. And some were akin to the ramblings of a tiny psychopath, like accidentally eating a poisonous lizard, being swallowed by a Venus flytrap and drowning in quicksand.

Dean beckoned to Lucien and he stiffened, expecting Dean to introduce him to the kids or invite him to talk to them as a group like he had. But Dean didn't—he just split the children into small groups and started to demonstrate how to use a bandage.

After a moment of watching Dean, Lucien took his own group of children and did the same. Over the next hour they covered how to clean and bandage small cuts and grazes, how to cool burns and scalds, and how to deal with nose bleeds. It all went surprisingly smoothly. And, frankly, it was a wonder they'd never done this before. Lucien had to concede that Dean's London surgery might not have been so bad after all.

After the demonstration the children were told it was break time, but most of them stayed in the hall. Dean was immediately surrounded by dozens of kids, some practically trying to climb him. Lucien stepped back, emotionally exhausted after having spoken to so many people, and folded himself down on to a long bench that sat against the wall, much too low for his tall frame.

One little girl approached Lucien by herself

and sat down next to him, eating her lunch quietly. After a moment she held out her open crisp packet to Lucien, offering him a crisp. He took one wordlessly, and gave her a smile before eating it.

Then Rafael barrelled up to Lucien and stopped himself at the last second, his hands braced against Lucien's knees. 'Hi, Mia,' he panted, addressing the girl next to Lucien. Then, 'Lucien, come and see my friends.'

'I can see them all from here.'

'Okay…' Rafael turned around to look at everyone and used Lucien's leg as a leaning post.

'Your dad's good at this, isn't he?' said Lucien.

'At what?'

'Teaching people how to do things.'

'He's not a teacher! He's a doctor!'

Lucien couldn't really argue with that, so he dropped the subject.

'My favourite bit of today was when you taught us how to tie a sling,' Rafael said.

'It was?'

He'd thought Dean's groups had certainly seemed to have much more fun than Lucien's. And he couldn't blame them.

'Yeah. I like the way you explain stuff. And you don't make embarrassing dad jokes.'

Lucien huffed a laugh. 'Don't tell Dean they're embarrassing.'

'He knows. That's why he does it!'

Rafael looked disgusted, which made Lucien laugh again.

Dean looked over, perhaps hearing Lucien laughing. Lucien's gaze met his for a moment, and they shared a shy smile.

Dean threw his work clothes into his bedroom hamper and showered quickly, then pulled on some soft grey sweatpants and a comfy T-shirt. He wanted to get started on cooking early, so all three of them could eat together and perhaps get rid of the residual tension that was hanging between the two of them.

They'd been sharing the house for several days now, but still kept mostly to their own rooms. The atmosphere between them was much less frosty than it had been, but there was still an awkwardness that Dean wasn't sure would ever disappear.

Dean's heart had been warmed by seeing Lucien at the school. He'd been reluctant with the children at first, but they'd loved him. It was probably the way he spoke to them like adults—he didn't temper his language or talk down to them.

Dean was planning to make his special spaghetti Bolognese. Rafael loved it, and so did everyone he made it for. Although it suddenly occurred to him that Lucien could be a vegan for all he knew. He tried to remember what was in the fridge downstairs, and if he'd seen any meat in there.

Lucien hadn't showed up at home yet, even though they'd both finished work at about the same time. Hopefully he hadn't arranged to go out and eat somewhere else.

'You okay in there?' Dean called as he passed the half-open bathroom door.

'I can manage to use the bathroom by myself, thank you.'

Dean smiled. Rafael was adorable when he got all prim and self-righteous. 'Good work, buddy. Are you okay if I go down to the kitchen?'

'Yes!'

'See you down there in a minute.'

Dean heard Rafael grumbling to himself as he headed off to the stairs. And just as Dean reached the ground floor Lucien arrived home. He shook off his umbrella over the doormat.

'When did it start raining?' asked Dean.

'About five seconds after I left the opticians. And about five minutes before I remembered I had an umbrella.'

'You should call me next time. I'll come and pick you up in the car…save you getting wet.'

Lucien's hair was soaked, and tiny rivulets of water ran down into his eyes as he ruffled it dry with a hand.

'So that's why you're late? You had an eye test?'

'No.' Lucien looked at Dean with a puzzled expression. 'I was just picking up my new frames. Did I arrange to meet you here or something?'

'No, no. Nothing like that. I just thought it would be cool if I cooked for us all.'

Lucien put down his bag and shrugged off his coat. 'You cook?'

'If there's one thing you should know about me, it's that I'm an excellent cook.'

'And so modest.'

'Is there anything you don't eat?'

'No, I'll eat whatever anyone makes for me. I can't cook at all.'

Dean waited for Lucien to hang up his coat, then took his arm and directed him into the kitchen. He loved a challenge.

'You can be my sous chef.'

'Didn't you hear me? I burn water.'

Dean sat Lucien down on one of the stools. 'I can teach anyone. You'll be great.'

Dean got the spaghetti out, then a pack of minced beef and a bottle of red wine, and set them on the table. Then he collected chopped tomatoes, onions, carrots, tomato puree and olive oil from various cupboards.

Lucien looked at all the ingredients in consternation. 'I didn't know we had any of that.'

'I got it all at lunchtime.' Dean grabbed a wedge of Parmesan from the fridge. 'Your first job is to grate this.' He paused. 'Do we even have a cheese grater?'

'I think so…' Lucien got up and pulled open the wide drawer next to the sink. 'My grandmother gave me a box of kitchen stuff years ago. I've never really used any of it.'

Dean joined him and looked into the drawer. He gasped at the array of delights like a kid at Christmas.

'Look at all this cool stuff! There's a box of professional kitchen knives in here. Do you know how much they cost?' Dean had been pining for a set like that for months, but couldn't justify the expense. He lifted them out. 'This is awesome. Can I use them?'

Lucien shrugged. 'Go for your life.'

Dean, way more thrilled than he should be over kitchen utensils, unpacked a couple of the knives, rinsed them under the tap, then dried them carefully. He got down his thick wooden chopping board and tried one of the knives out on the onion, groaning happily at how clean the cut was.

'Oh, my God…'

Lucien gave him a funny look. 'It can't be *that* stimulating.'

'You don't know.'

Lucien shook his head indulgently, and sat down with the cheese grater.

Dean pushed a plate over to him. 'Grate about half of it on there. I like a lot of cheese.'

'Noted.'

Lucien did as he was told. He was a much easier student than Rafael, who found it necessary to ask about fifteen questions before completing any task. Dean wouldn't have him any other way, though. And he was proud of him. The kid had mastered a lot of basic cooking skills in just the few months they'd been living together.

Thinking of Rafael seemed to conjure him into the room. He wandered into the kitchen dragging his battered cuddly dinosaur along the floor with one hand, clutching an action figure in the other.

'Hi, Lucien.'

'What am I, chopped liver?' asked Dean.

'I said hi to you already.'

Rafael dropped the dinosaur, pulled himself up on to the stool, then gazed expectantly at Lucien.

Lucien turned to Dean, confused.

'He wants his colouring pens—they're up on the shelf. Could you get them? My hands are all oniony.'

Dean went back to his chopping, but kept one eye on them to see how Lucien would respond. Lucien paused, wiped his hands on a tea towel, then stood and gathered the neat stack of paper and coloured pens that Dean had tidied away the night before. He deposited them gently on to the table by Rafael, then looked back at Dean questioningly, as if to ask if he'd done it right.

Dean smiled.

Yes, it was a small thing, but sometimes you had to start small.

Rafael reached for the pens and started scribbling. 'Is dinner ready yet?' he asked.

'As you can see, we're just cooking it. It'll be a while, but it's your favourite,' answered Dean.

'Lasagne?' Rafael asked excitedly.

'Okay, your second favourite.'

'Cool, I like all my favourites.'

'Why did you decide to cook for me today?' Lucien asked Dean. 'Any special reason?'

'It's an apology dinner.'

'Why?' Lucien looked up suspiciously. 'What did you do?'

'The accidental videoing.'

'Oh, that.'

'And roping you into the school visit. I know it's not normally your kind of thing.'

'No apology necessary.'

'Why? Because you secretly loved it?'

Dean winked at Lucien, and he swore Lucien's cheeks went pink.

'I wouldn't go that far.'

'But you didn't hate it?'

Suddenly Dean was worried. Maybe Lucien wanted to be alone…maybe Dean should stop teasing him and give him some space. Although surely Lucien would go up to his office if he really didn't want to be talked to.

Lucien smiled, although he seemed to be trying to hide it, and Dean's tension settled.

'It made a nice change, I suppose.'

'I'm glad,' said Dean.

Lucien finished grating and shook the last

flakes off the grater on to the plate. 'Some of those children were very unusual.'

Dean shrugged. 'Kids are.'

'Half the things they said were completely illogical. And the Venus flytrap obsession…?'

Dean laughed. 'You say illogical—I say imaginative. Don't you remember being a kid and thinking the greatest dangers you would face in adult life would be killer plants, giant whirlpools and quicksand?'

'I can't say I do.'

Dean smiled. He couldn't imagine Lucien as a kid. Just as a tiny version of himself, with suede elbows on a tiny jacket, carrying a mini brown leather briefcase.

'I thought you said you were bad with kids,' said Dean, tipping the chopped onion into a large pan and adding some crushed garlic.

'I am.'

'Didn't look that way to me… Looked like you connected with them pretty well.'

Lucien shrugged shyly. 'What should I prepare next?'

Dean handed him a carrot. 'Maybe you've had some practice with a relative's kids? Or a girlfriend's?'

Lucien raised an eyebrow at Dean. 'I don't have girlfriends, Dean.'

Dean nodded. 'Gotcha.'

'And there are no children in my family—

at least none that I spend time around.' Lucien looked at Rafael, who was now colouring in what looked like an elephant with a green pen. 'They are a totally alien species to me.'

'Hear that, Raf?' said Dean. 'He called you an alien.'

Rafael looked up indignantly. 'I'm not an alien!'

'Dean,' Lucien admonished sternly, raising an eyebrow, and making Dean's heart rate quicken. 'Stop getting me in trouble.'

Dean swallowed hard. Lucien being authoritative should not be that sexy.

'Raf? Why don't you go and watch TV on the sofa in the living room? Then you can spread out your stuff on the coffee table.'

'Okay!' Rafael gathered up all his pens and paper and hurried off to watch the big screen TV.

'He loves your TV,' Dean told Lucien.

Lucien smiled. 'Glad someone does. I hardly ever use it.'

Their hands touched accidentally as they both reached for the vegetable peeler. Dean flushed and busied himself stirring the onions. Lucien glared at his carrot as he awkwardly peeled it.

'Didn't your girlfriend mind you moving out of London?' he asked.

Dean side-eyed him. 'What girlfriend?'

'I just thought… I mean… I've gathered that you and Rafael's mother were apart for a long time? So you might be in a new relationship now?'

Dean nodded, unsure of how to respond. 'I've been single for a while.'

That was the second part of Lucien's question covered. Now for the first part. Maybe he could just gloss over it? He was such an idiot... He hadn't thought to prepare in advance what he would tell Lucien about himself and Rafael's mother. What was safe to share without revealing his secret? How should he handle this? He'd rather tell Lucien as much of the truth as possible, considering the big lie that was at the centre of all this.

'I was never really with Rafael's mother at all.'

Dean glanced into the living room at Rafael, but he was happily watching the television, pen in hand, about to get ink all over his knee if he didn't start paying attention to it. Regardless, he was well out of earshot and wouldn't hear whatever Dean was about to say, or not say.

Lucien frowned. 'You weren't?' His face cleared after a moment and he continued quietly, 'So Rafael was the result of a one-night stand?'

Dean paused. 'Yes, that's true.'

'And after his mother passed away Rafael came to you?'

'Yes.'

'I'm sorry for your loss,' Lucien murmured. 'I don't think I've said that yet.'

'Thank you. She was my best friend.'

Lucien seemed to make a move to reach for

Dean's hand, but he aborted it at the last moment and put his hands in his lap.

Even now, talking about Charlotte made Dean's eyes sting. And the sweet, genuine look on Lucien's face wasn't helping. Dean felt so guilty for concealing the truth. Part of him wanted to shout it out there and then: *You're Rafael's father!* But he couldn't. It was imperative that he put Rafael's safety first. He had to keep quiet about it just a little longer.

'Can I ask something else?' said Lucien.

'Sure.'

Dean gave himself a metaphorical shake and made himself smile. He took the peeled carrot from Lucien and chopped it, still marvelling at the sharpness of the knife.

'Not that it's any of my business,' Lucien continued. 'Actually, forget it.'

Dean laughed. 'Lucien, you can ask me anything. I'm an open book, buddy.'

'Well… I've noticed that Rafael calls you Dean. I must admit, I did wonder why. But, as I say, it's absolutely none of my business.'

Oh.

Dean's stomach swirled with sudden nerves. How could Dean not have realised that would raise questions? He was so used to Rafael calling him Dean that it hadn't occurred to him that it might sound strange to other people. It looked as if he'd have to come clean about a little more than he had planned.

Dean took a deep breath. 'Technically, I'm his legal guardian—not a blood relation.'

'Oh,' said Lucien, gazing at him thoughtfully.

Dean steeled himself for judgement, or more difficult questions. Or even some anger that he'd bent the truth a few moments ago.

'I'm surprised. He looks just like you.'

'He does?' Dean's heart soared at that, and he wasn't sure why.

'He has your freckles! And that dimple. And the ability to be infuriatingly cheeky and endearing at the same time.'

'Oh, really?'

Lucien avoided Dean's gaze and bit his lip.

Dean chuckled softly. 'I was around him a lot when he was born,' Dean said. 'His mother and I knew each other for years. She was amazing. You know, she could—' Dean cut himself off. If he gave too many details Lucien might somehow recognise Charlotte from his description.

He'd been about to explain how Charlotte could play any song you wanted on the piano by ear, without sheet music. But if he told Lucien that he might also tell him about how she could somehow bake anything, with no recipe and no measuring, just by instinct. And how she could make up the best bedtime story you'd ever heard off the top of her head.

Despite all that, she'd never thought she was anything special. Dean had never met anyone quite like her, and he never would again. He didn't mean to romanticise her perfection now she was gone, or forget all her flaws, but with Charlotte there weren't many to forget. She truly was the kindest, funniest person he'd ever known, and it broke his heart that Rafael wouldn't get all those years he deserved to spend with her.

Rafael had indeed been the result of an impulsive one-night stand at the end of Charlotte's medical training. It had always been a running joke between them that the one solitary time in her life that she'd ever slept with a man she'd managed to get pregnant. Charlotte had already arranged to move hundreds of miles away from the southern town where she and the father had trained for her first position in medicine, and she hadn't thought he would be interested. Besides, she'd been perfectly happy to raise her child alone.

She'd never really talked about the father much. And Dean hadn't given the man a second thought until a few months ago.

Lucien was still waiting for Dean to continue, his gaze soft and encouraging.

'One night I went to bed and everything was perfectly normal. Then I was woken up by a phone call and my whole world changed. My friend was dead and apparently she'd mentioned me in her will. I was thinking she'd left me a book or a letter. But it wasn't.'

'It was Rafael?'

Dean nodded. 'It was a huge shock at the time, but I'm so glad she did. I love him so much…'

Lucien smiled, and Dean found himself continuing. Even though he'd never really felt comfortable talking about this to anyone else.

'When someone has a baby they always say that when they hold it for the first time this unfathomable tidal wave of primal love rushes through them, and they know they would die for them immediately.'

Lucien nodded.

'I didn't know that could happen to me. With a kid who wasn't even mine. But the first time I held him—' Dean shook his head. 'I knew that I'd die for him, kill for him, raze cities to the ground… All that good stuff.'

'I can see that.'

Lucien's gaze ran over Dean's face and stopped on his mouth for a second. Dean swallowed and looked away. He hadn't meant to open up quite that much, but something about Lucien made him want to be honest. Maybe it was Lucien's quiet manner…the way he gazed at Dean, just listening, waiting for him to say more. Not trying to jump in with his own words, never just talking for the sake of it. And when he did speak it meant something.

The sauce was nearly done, so Dean threw some fresh spaghetti into a pan of boiling water. It would only take a few minutes to cook.

'So anyway… To double back to your initial question. There's no partner back in London.'

'I see. I suppose having a child must make dating harder.'

'Oh, I'm not even thinking about dating any more.'

'Why not?' asked Lucien. 'Is it hard to find the time? Or babysitters?'

Lucien side-eyed Dean quickly, and Dean smiled. Lucien's face was so easy to read. Dean would bet money that he was very much hoping not to be asked to babysit.

'It's not that,' he said. 'I just think my dating years are over.'

Lucien shocked him by laughing.

'What?' asked Dean.

'Oh, I didn't mean to laugh at you. It's just you said that like an eighty-year-old who's just become a widower. I think you have a few years left in you yet, Dean.'

Dean shook his head, amused at Lucien's laughter. 'Nah. I'm just not into casual dating any more. You can't really do that with a kid in tow. And I'm clearly not husband material. So that leaves me nowhere.'

'Who says you're not husband material?'

Dean shrugged. 'Everyone.'

He'd never really thought about it before. It was just something he accepted about himself. Ever since he was a child, people had found it easy to leave him. He was likeable, but not loveable. People wanted to date him once or twice, but rarely anything more.

'People don't see me as a long-term prospect,' he said now. 'My longest relationship was six months. She dumped me to get back with her ex. And the longest before that was only four. He left me when he met someone better. I'm just not the sort of person people think of in terms of for ever.'

Lucien frowned at him for a long moment. 'Well, you have a son now. That's for ever.'

Dean smiled. 'He's the only long-term relationship I need.'

'He's a great kid.'

'You think? You like him?'

Lucien nodded. 'Of course. He's very…surprising.'

Dean called Rafael and they sat down to eat together around the kitchen counter. Lucien set out a knife, fork and plate neatly for Rafael without Dean even having to ask.

Dean served up the food, giving Lucien the biggest plateful. Then he eyed Rafael trying to twist spaghetti on to his fork and placed a large pile of napkins near his plate.

Dean had practically told Lucien his entire life story. How had that ended up happening? He was just so easy to talk to. But maybe it was time to change the subject.

'So, everyone at work today was talking about a charity auction?'

'What?' said Lucien. He coughed and grabbed a napkin to wipe his mouth. 'Oh, no, that's not a thing.'

'Seemed an awful lot like a thing to me.'

'Well, I wouldn't know, because I don't get involved with it.'

'So they said.'

'Oh, I bet they did. What exactly did they say?'

'That you're a big Scrooge and that the charity would probably make double the money if only you joined in.'

'I don't see how.'

Dean smiled. Lucien really was endearing when he was grumpy or evasive. 'So what do they mean? What is this auction about?'

Lucien shook his head. 'It's so ridiculous…'

'Tell me.'

'It's practically medieval. I assume they were trying to get you involved?'

Dean nodded. 'I asked what I could do to help, and they told me to get you on board.'

Lucien rolled his eyes so hard they almost fell out of his head.

'But I still don't really know what they want us to do,' Dean finished.

'I'll tell you what they want us to do…'

Lucien was getting more animated by the second, fuelled apparently by indignation. He reached into his back pocket and got out his glasses, slipping them on before he continued.

'They want to parade us around on stage and get rich local women to bid on us like cattle.'

Dean wasn't prepared for how attractive Lucien would be wearing glasses. He stared a little before he remembered how to speak. 'Like cattle, huh?'

'Exactly. A meat market.'

'Start from the beginning—I'm not following.'

Lucien sighed. 'It's this big charity event that takes place every year. It's been going on for decades. My grandmother runs it. *But*—' Lucien held up one finger resolutely '—that does not make it my responsibility to take part.'

'No, buddy.' Dean nodded along. 'Of course not.'

Lucien looked at Dean in surprise. 'Well, you're the only person that agrees with me. Anyway, they ask me every year to be involved, and every year I say no and write a very nice cheque to assuage my guilt.'

'But what do they want you to do?'

'They make people line up on stage and then they go along the line one by one as members of the public bid on them for dates.'

That all sounded very innocuous to Dean, but Lucien obviously found the idea utterly horrific.

'Oh, God,' said Lucien, 'it's probably your idea of fun.'

Dean smiled. 'I mean, it doesn't sound so terrible to me. People bid, everyone has a good laugh, the charity gets some money. And then you spend a couple of hours on a faux date with someone you don't know…probably have an okay time and maybe make a new friend. That's not so bad, is it?'

Lucien had a look of shocked disgust on his face. 'How are we even the same species?'

'Okay, describe it to me from your point of view.'

'First of all, what if no one bids on you? That would be mortifying.'

Lucien's gaze ran over Dean's face, possibly lingering on his lips again for a nano second, but Dean couldn't be sure.

'Obviously that wouldn't happen to you, but try to imagine the concept in the far reaches of your imagination.'

Dean laughed. Lucien was funny when he was sarcastic.

'Okay, yes, that would be embarrassing,' Dean admitted. 'But you can't think that would happen to you?'

'Of course it would.' Lucien looked at him as if he was crazy. 'Second of all, hundreds of people are staring at you, expecting you to perform for them or something. Hideous. Plus you could trip or fall at any moment.'

'Not if you're careful.'

Lucien had never said so much at once, and Dean was delighted.

'And, worst of all, the second you're on stage in front of a crowd you're being judged,' Lucien continued. '*That's the outfit he chose for this? He thinks his hair looks good like that? He thinks this is appropriate behaviour for a doctor?* No, as a matter of fact, I don't—' He suddenly seemed to remember Dean was there listening to him and finished his passionate rant rather quietly. 'Yeah, so that's why I always say no.'

'Have you ever actually been to the charity auction? Maybe it's not as bad as you think.'

'I haven't been for a few years, but I used to go when I was younger. Now I stay at home, with a locked door between me and anyone who might think it wise to try and drag me into it at the last minute.'

'Like who?'

'Have you met Helen? Plus my grandmother isn't great at understanding the word *no* when it comes to these sorts of things. I'm amazed I've managed to argue her down all these years, to be honest.'

Dean pushed some dislodged spaghetti back on to Rafael's plate with his fork. 'Now, don't get cross with me, Lucien. But, speaking of Helen,

I did promise her I'd try to convince you to take part this year.'

'Dean!'

Dean stopped. 'You've finally called me Dean, instead of Dr Vasquez.'

'Sorry, I—'

'Don't be an idiot. I *want* you to call me Dean. We do live together, after all.'

Lucien nodded and looked down at his plate.

Rafael's plate was mostly clean, so Dean wiped Rafael's face with a wet cloth and sent him upstairs to get ready for bed. He knew that in ten minutes he'd go upstairs to check on him and find that he'd been reading or playing Nintendo Switch the whole time, but that was their routine, and they both liked it that way.

'So, now Raf's gone, do you want some adult dessert?' asked Dean.

'I dread to think what makes it "adult".'

Dean laughed. 'It just has rum in it.'

He pulled open the fridge and took out two glass bowls of dessert and a bar of seventy percent cocoa cooking chocolate.

'They're premade. We just have to add chocolate flakes on top.'

Dean grabbed one of Lucien's new knives and unwrapped the chocolate.

Lucien watched. 'Can I do it?'

Dean hesitated, he wasn't sure about Lucien's knife skills, and the blade was insanely sharp, but

Lucien looked so eager to help that he couldn't say no.

Dean handed over the knife. 'Okay. But be careful.' Dean placed the dark chocolate on to the wooden chopping board. 'Just slice it thinly into chunks. We don't need all that much. Unless you particularly love chocolate?'

Lucien looked up. 'What kind of man do you take me for? Of course I particularly love chocolate.'

'Then go at it.'

He did. And within seconds cursed under his breath and dropped the knife, letting it clatter to the table.

Damn it, Dean should have listened to his instincts. Since having a son, he'd found his sixth sense for danger had sharpened considerably, and was rarely inaccurate.

'What have you done?'

'I cut myself.' Lucien examined his finger. 'But it's fine.'

Blood dripped down Lucien's hand on to the chopping board.

'Come here.'

Dean took Lucien's wrist and led him around the table to the sink. Lucien followed without question and let Dean push his hand under the cold tap. He held it firmly under the water for a moment.

'It's not too deep. Shouldn't need stitches.'

Dean wrapped some paper towel around Lucien's finger and pressed it firmly. 'Wait here.'

Dean ran to the bathroom and returned to Lucien with a red and blue Spiderman plaster. 'Sorry, it's all I have.'

Lucien let him wrap it around his finger. 'This is ironic,' he said.

'How?'

'The very same day we lecture children on how to bandage cuts…'

'True. Oh, Raf's gonna be gutted he missed out on putting your arm in a sling.'

'Maybe tomorrow.' Lucien smiled.

Dean realised it was probably time to stop patting Lucien's arm and let him have his hand back.

'What if they did something different this year?' he asked.

Lucien gazed at him questioningly.

'At the auction. Maybe they could take the dating aspect out of it. They could offer other things.'

'Like what?'

'Like if the person being auctioned didn't want a date, they could offer some other prize instead.'

'I don't have the first clue what prize I could give anyone. Free GP consultations for a month?'

'They're free already.'

'A box of latex gloves? A stethoscope? A special chair in the waiting room?'

'Lucien! Think outside the box.'

'I don't know what that means.'

'Something that's not related to the practice.'

'Oh.'

'There's a concept!' Dean teased. 'What do you do outside of work?'

'Absolutely nothing.'

'There must be something,' Dean encouraged.

Lucien adjusted his glasses. 'I read books. I study bees. And I go rock climbing.'

'You climb rocks?' Dean asked.

'Yes.'

'As in cliff faces, ropes, abseiling, crampons?'

'That about covers it.'

'Oh.' Dean stared at him hard, then looked him up and down slowly.

'You seem confused?' said Lucien.

'No. No, I just… I didn't know you did anything like that. You're full of surprises, aren't you?' he murmured quietly. 'So, if I clear it with Helen, instead of a date, maybe you could give someone a climbing lesson?'

Lucien frowned. 'I suppose I could do that, yes.'

'Sounds good to me!' Dean wrote a note in his phone. 'We're coming back to that bee thing later, too.'

CHAPTER FOUR

DEAN BURST INTO Lucien's home office just after seven p.m. 'Rafael's out of Frosty Stars. If he doesn't have them in the morning he'll be unbearable. I have half an hour before the shop shuts, so I'm running out to get some. God, I hope they have it. Can you watch him? He's downstairs in front of the TV.'

Lucien barely had time to process Dean's garbled monologue before Dean had whirled off down the stairs, pulling on his jacket.

'Okay,' Lucien shouted. 'But don't be long!'

'I'll only be ten minutes!'

'This is most unsatisfactory,' Lucien said to the cat, who until then had been sleeping quite comfortably on Lucien's lap.

Binxie leapt down to the floor and stood in the doorway, looking after Dean. The front door slammed, and Binxie turned back to Lucien to chirrup.

After last night, Lucien felt a lot closer to Dean. He'd even been given answers to some of the questions that had been floating around his mind for days. But now he had new questions. Dean wasn't related to Rafael by blood, but he'd been tasked with raising him. He could only assume that perhaps the biological father was deceased, or a horribly unsuitable person.

But he'd already pushed Dean to answer enough personal questions—he certainly didn't want to push further. So he'd just have to wonder.

Dean had not stopped surprising him. First he'd learned that Dean wasn't the over-confident egotist that Lucien had first assumed. He had the capability to be shy and to doubt himself. And it had stunned Lucien to learn that Dean had such a low opinion of himself and his attractiveness as a partner.

Admittedly, Lucien had only known him a few days. But when he had so stupidly cut himself chopping chocolate, Dean hadn't mocked him or left him to take care of himself. That was probably the father in him. He seemed to thrive on looking after other people. Not an uncommon trait in a doctor, but Lucien had known a lot of doctors, and few were as warm and caring as Dean seemed to be.

Binxie put her front paws on Lucien's knee and licked his hand.

'You like him, huh?' Lucien put his book away and Binxie mewed. 'Yes, I'm sure he's very nice. But I'm the one who feeds you. Remember that.'

Not having had younger siblings, or nieces and nephews, Lucien wasn't exactly sure what watching Rafael meant. Was he simply required to be an available adult in the house that Rafael could come to for help were it needed? Or was he supposed to literally watch him? And how had he got to this age without knowing this sort of thing?

Lucien gave Binxie a head-rub, the furry little traitor, then rearranged a pile of papers on his desk. 'Okay, Binx, you're right. Now I'm simply hiding from the child. Let's go down. How bad can it be?'

It was probably best to err on the side of caution and keep an actual eye on him.

Lucien felt half panicked and half flattered that Dean trusted him to look after his child. Maybe not half and half...perhaps more of a sixty-forty split on the side of panic. Or ninety-ten.

Lucien headed down, followed by Binxie. Which in cat terms meant weaving between Lucien's legs all the way down, cutting him off at every corner and generally trying to trip him at every opportunity. Which made no evolutionary sense. For if Lucien lay dead in a crumpled heap at the foot of the stairs Binxie would have no one to open her bags of gourmet cat food or scratch her under the chin. But Binxie's strengths didn't lie in logic.

Lucien found Rafael curled up on the sofa, watching what looked like a horrifically violent superhero film on television. Had he switched over to this the second Dean left? Or was this sanctioned viewing?

Lucien hesitated at the door, then sidled in and sank on to the other end of the sofa. 'What are you watching?'

'It's the best bit of *Iron Man*. Loki throws him out of a window, but his exoskeleton armour jumps out too and saves him.'

'Ah…' Lucien nodded, not having a clue what half those words meant.

'Do you like Iron Man?' asked Rafael.

'I don't really know much about him, to be honest.'

'Really?' Rafael looked gobsmacked. 'Who's your favourite superhero?'

Lucien cast his mind back to the last time he'd cared about superheroes. He'd probably been the same age as Rafael. 'I guess I like Superman?'

Rafael nodded. 'Yeah, that makes sense. You kind of look like him.'

Lucien decided to take that puzzling comment as a compliment. 'What superhero do you look like?'

'Hmm…' Rafael grabbed a cushion and hugged it as he thought. 'There aren't many kid heroes. But maybe Wiccan? He's in Marvel. He's cool.'

'And which is Dean like?'

'Oh, he's Captain America. Cause he's so strong and smart and stuff.'

Lucien nodded, and wondered what to say next.

Rafael stared around the room. 'You have a lot of books.'

'Yes, I suppose I do. But I'm not the only one. I saw your dad unpacking a lot of books when you moved in.'

All the boxes he'd walked past on the stairs that first day had seemed to be stacked full of things for Rafael. Dean didn't seem to have brought many of his own belongings in comparison.

'You have like a whole library.'

The child sounded a little in awe. And Lucien couldn't believe he was about to say this, but… 'If you're careful, you can read anything you want.'

'I can?' Rafael stared at him open-mouthed. 'Dean said I wasn't allowed to touch anything.'

'Oh, well, he wasn't to know. Books are made to be read, you know? And shared.'

'Wow.'

Rafael jumped down off the sofa, TV forgotten for a moment, and started looking through the lower shelves. And Lucien was strangely okay with it. No one had ever shown an interest in his books. He had a lot of non-fiction filled with big glossy pictures. Books about palaeontology, bugs, butterflies, space and maps.

With some difficulty, Rafael pulled out a large, heavy book about the beetles of Asia, and was soon marvelling over the gigantic close-up photographs of iridescent gold beetles and bright purple-horned stags.

This wasn't going so badly. It was easier to hold a conversation with Rafael than he'd thought it would be. Usually Lucien felt as if people were judging what he said, but Rafael just went with the flow unquestioningly, and Lucien felt he could say anything, however silly or pointless, and Rafael wouldn't think he was odd. The boy seemed remarkably well adjusted for having been through such a trauma at an early age. He was fortunate to have a dad like Dean.

'This beetle is the best one.' Rafael pointed at a glossy blue and green beetle with a ferocious horn and spiny legs, and grinned up at Lucien.

Lucien smiled. 'Great choice. That's the Asiatic Rhinoceros beetle.'

It was one of Lucien's favourites too. He was proud of Rafael for noticing how special it was. Suddenly Lucien wanted to impart every bit of knowledge he had that Rafael might find interesting. He shifted closer to Rafael and turned a couple of pages in the book. There was one specimen he remembered being obsessed with when he was Rafael's age.

'You'll love this one...'

Rafael read out the name of the beetle Lucien pointed to and cackled. Then he moved the book on to both their laps and hugged Lucien's arm tightly. 'You're funny.'

Lucien had never been so disarmed in all his life. He cuddled Binxie all the time, but she never hugged back. He never really let anyone else close enough for hugs. The last person to hug him must have been his grandmother, at his mother's funeral, and even that had been under duress.

Lucien sighed as he identified the emotion he was currently feeling. It was fondness. He'd allowed himself to become fond of Rafael, and even Dean. This was literally the opposite of everything he'd planned. But he knew there was no turning back now. You couldn't flick a switch and stop feeling affection. If he could do that he never would have kept Binxie after she'd shown up tiny, mewling and soaking wet one stormy night. He could have given her to a shelter any time in the first week or two after he'd let her into the house. But he'd fed her, and talked to her, and she'd purred on his lap and he'd become fond.

But a cat was very different from two human beings. If he opened his heart and his life to them things would get very complicated. As adorable as Rafael was, and as attracted to Dean as he might be becoming, that didn't change the fact that people got hurt when Lucien allowed himself to get distracted by his personal life. His ex and his mother were proof of that. And the only solution for that was simply not to have one.

He'd allowed Rafael and Dean in too much already.

Dean wandered up and down the small cereal aisle at the local mini supermarket. Luckily, they did have Rafael's Frosty Stars. Dean grabbed a box off the shelf and carried it under his arm. Of course there had been plenty left for Rafael to eat in the morning until Dean himself had polished them off. But he'd needed plausible deniability. And a reason to duck out of the house for ten minutes.

How else could he gently test out Lucien's progress with Rafael? It wasn't a big test—he just wanted to see how they got on without him there as a buffer. Would Dean get home to find Lucien had stayed upstairs in his room? Would he have forgotten he was supposed to be watching Rafael altogether? Dean didn't think so, but he didn't know for sure. He trusted Lucien not to go out and abandon Rafael, of course, or he would never have left Rafael with him.

The shop was small and bright. The fluorescent strip light above flashed on and off minutely, and made Dean feel faintly nauseous. The tinny music playing through the speakers wasn't great, but at least it was quiet.

'Hello, Doctor!'

Of course, having left the house for only a few minutes, he would have to run in to one of his patients. Such was the beauty of a small town. Dean plastered a smile on his face and turned around.

It was the man who'd been kicked by the angry cow.

'Fancy seeing you here,' the man said, grinning.

'Well, it is the only shop in town.'

Dean took the offered hand and shook it warmly.

'Fair point. Run out of cereal, did you?'

Dean laughed politely.

'Not a very healthy choice for a doctor.'

'It's my son's favourite. Apparently he can't live without it.'

As Dean had learned from some rather distressing tantrums early on in their relationship. He grabbed a chocolate bar for Rafael too, feeling a bit guilty for using his son as a Lucien test.

In his short wait in the queue, he managed to be spotted by a second patient from that day's surgery, and then smoothly deflected a request to look at a rash on the checkout lady's neck. After encouraging the poor woman to make an appointment with him at the surgery, Dean finally got away.

Those interactions might have made him feel frustrated back in London. He had always been trying desperately to get home, or get to work.

Wherever he was, he'd always been supposed to be somewhere else. But here he felt he had time for these people. This was what his job was all about.

And, as out of place as he had felt at first, and as dangerous as it was to let himself want this, maybe this was exactly where he was supposed to be…

Dean stepped out into the fresh, warm breeze and glanced at his watch. With the two-minute walk back home, it was time to get going. His stomach churned on the walk back, and he felt weirdly anxious as he turned the key in the lock and let himself into the kitchen. He left the cereal and chocolate on the counter and found Rafael and Lucien in the living room.

What he saw dissolved all his worries and warmed his heart.

Lucien and Rafael sat closely on the sofa, a huge book open over both their laps. Rafael was giggling at something Lucien had said. After a minute, Lucien looked over his shoulder and noticed Dean watching them. His face seemed to go through a number of emotions, then he sighed and stood, taking the book with him.

'Did you get the cereal?'

Dean nodded. 'You look like you're having fun.'

Lucien looked down at Rafael and gently passed

him the book. 'I've got work I really need to get back to.'

Lucien strode past Dean and disappeared up the stairs.

Dean took his place on the sofa, feeling deflated, and put an arm around Rafael. 'What have you got there, buddy?'

'It's about bugs. It has really cool pictures.'

Rafael seemed quiet. 'What were you two laughing at before?' asked Dean.

'Lucien was telling me about the dung beetle.' Rafael paused. 'Did I do something wrong to make him go?'

'No, of course not. I think Lucien has some important work to do.'

Dean distracted Rafael with the chocolate and felt awful. Lucien's hot and cold routine was fine when it was directed at Dean, but not acceptable when it hurt Rafael. Was Dean right to worry after all? Was Lucien not dad material? It would be heartbreaking to have to leave now, so soon after he'd allowed himself to feel he might belong.

At work the next day, Helen slammed her clipboard on to Dean's desk, almost making him choke on his lunchtime baguette.

'I've added you two to the official auction schedule. So there's no backing out now.'

Dean nodded, coughing. 'No problem. We're both happy to help.'

'You'll have to tell me how you convinced Lucien to do it. That ability could prove very helpful to me in future.'

Dean laughed. 'We just talked about it and I found a way to make it less of a nightmare for him. Like I told you, shifting the focus off winning a date and on to winning a prize.'

Helen nodded. 'That was a pretty good idea—thank you for that. The auction board loved it. And even Lucien's grandmother thinks it'll give the whole event a bit of a rejuvenation.'

Helen quickly reapplied her lipstick in the small mirror hanging on the wall over Dean's printer.

'You don't fancy being auctioned off yourself?' Dean asked.

'If I was on stage, I wouldn't be able to look after Rafael for you, would I? And, not to give you a big head, but I think you'll pull a bigger audience than me.'

'Hey, no negative self-talk. Mr Helen is a lucky guy.'

Helen put her lipstick away and blotted her lips with a tissue. 'Quite right.'

Then she turned her focus on to Dean, and he could tell he wouldn't like what was coming.

'So, what about you?'

'What about me?' Dean responded.

'I might be wrong, but I don't believe there is a current Mr or Mrs Dean?'

'Correct.'

'Have you ever been involved with someone serious?'

Dean shrugged. 'Not really.'

Everyone Dean had loved had left him. His father. His mother, who'd tried her best but failed. Every one of his mother's boyfriends, who had paid him attention to impress her, but bailed on him eventually. As an adult, he'd never been short of dates, but that was all people thought he was good for or interested in. No one ever wanted to stay.

After so many years, he'd learned that the fewer people he allowed to get close to him, the less he could be hurt. He hid it with bravado, but he felt broken inside.

'Does that bother you?' asked Helen.

Normally Dean would laugh off a question like that and change the subject, but something made him pause. 'It never used to. But lately—I don't know. It might be nice to find the right one.'

Helen patted his arm. 'They're out there somewhere. Or maybe you've found them already?'

Lucien's face popped up in his mind and he blinked it away. 'I don't know about that. Sounds too good to be true.'

It really was time to change the subject now.

'Fancy a coffee?'

Helen tutted, but acquiesced, and Dean got her a cup from the machine, and himself a glass of cold tap water.

'So how long have you known Lucien?' Dean asked, once back at his desk.

Helen smiled wryly, and Dean realised he might not have changed the subject quite as smoothly as he'd hoped.

'For ever,' she answered. 'He had his first placement here.'

'Oh, wow—so you knew him back when he was a baby doctor?'

'I had to hold his hand through his first mid-consultation fainter, his first burst catheter and his first projectile vomiting baby.'

'I've been there...'

Dean smiled. It was strange to imagine Lucien as new and inexperienced.

'I still remember in his first few months on the job,' Helen continued, 'when my daughter was eleven, she broke her wrist and came to Lucien for a check-up. At the end of the consultation she asked him to her middle school prom.'

'No!'

'He was mortified, but a total gentleman. He let her down very gently.'

Dean laughed. That was adorable.

'So, you seem to be settling in very well. How are you finding country life, really?'

'Surprisingly good. I was nervous about it. About whether people would accept me or think I was out of my depth.'

'Or whether you'd find the place boring as all get out.'

'Not boring. Just different. And it is. But I kind of love it. And it's so much better for Raf. He already loves it here. Acts like he's never lived anywhere else.'

'I must say you are doing remarkably well at this dad thing.'

'Well, I'm getting there. Doing my best.'

Dean always felt self-conscious when people gave him compliments about being a father. He didn't feel he'd earned them yet. Or that he even knew what he was doing, half the time.

Helen grinned. 'You're doing better than you think you are. Now, get back to work.'

CHAPTER FIVE

ON AUCTION DAY, Helen dropped around to collect Rafael.

'You remember Helen?' said Dean. 'The lady I work with?' Rafael nodded shyly as Helen waved down at him. 'She's going to take you to play on the bouncy castle outside the town hall, then after that she'll go with you to the auction, and we'll meet you there later.'

'After our ritual humiliation,' Lucien cut in.

As soon as Dean said 'bouncy castle' Rafael's eyes lit up, and he pulled on Helen's sleeve, propelling her towards the hall.

'Okay, take it easy,' Dean called. 'You be good for Helen, like we talked about, and do everything she asks.'

'Okay!' Rafael answered, still running.

'Raf!' Dean yelled, stopping Rafael in his tracks by the front door. Dean knelt down and pointed to his cheek. 'Don't I get a kiss goodbye?'

Rafael rushed at him, gave him a quick hug,

then ran back to the front door and a grinning Helen. 'Bye, Daddy!'

Rafael was gone before Dean could fully process what Rafael had said. He remained kneeling on the floor and stared at the closed door in silence, his lips parted.

Lucien stepped closer. 'Was that the first time he's ever called you that?'

Dean nodded. His blood rushed in his ears and he felt as if he might explode. How could Rafael bless him with that gift and then just leave? What was he supposed to do with this rush of emotion? He felt as if he'd just jumped out of a plane at ten thousand feet. Who could he hug?

He turned to Lucien, a huge smile on his face, only to find a matching one on Lucien's. Which suddenly brought Dean smack back down to earth. Lucien was Rafael's father too. He deserved to hear that word from Rafael just as much as Dean—maybe even more.

Needing to hug Lucien now more than ever, he reached out, and Lucien let Dean pull him into his arms, holding him tight as Dean squeezed a silent apology into his shoulders.

'It felt that good, huh?' Lucien murmured, right by Dean's ear.

'You have no idea.'

The morning of the auction had dawned bright and terrifying. The dread had been heavy in Lucien's chest even before he was fully awake, but he'd sighed and dragged himself out of bed. He'd successfully avoided this auction for over a decade, but the second Dean came along he had managed to let himself get roped in.

What an idiot.

But now, standing in the hall with an armful of elated Dean, the day didn't seem so bad after all.

Lucien had intended to avoid Dean for a couple of days, embarrassed about the way he'd acted, and convinced they were getting too close. Dean had seemed a little standoffish himself—which was hardly surprising when Lucien had been so abrupt. But everything had changed after lunch the following day.

While Dean had been busy changing the oil in his car, Rafael had asked Lucien to make him pancakes. Now, when people said they could burn water, they were usually exaggerating, but with Lucien it was accurate. He could barely make toast without setting off the smoke alarm, and he normally stuck to eating ready meals from the mini supermarket or wolfing down a quick piece of toast.

But Rafael had gazed up at him with his big charcoal-grey eyes and a strange determination had come over Lucien. He would make this poor child pancakes if it killed him. And it very well might.

Anyway, cut to an hour later, and Lucien had

had two of Dean's cookbooks open on the counter, trying to combine two pancake recipes because he couldn't find all the ingredients for either one. He'd used every bowl and spoon in the house, and the table had been covered in spilled flour and broken eggs when Dean had finally found them. He'd stared at the mess, and at Rafael giggling, and at the flour Lucien had suspected he had on his cheek, with a small smile, before gently taking over. Within ten minutes they'd had a clean kitchen and a pile of pancakes each. Dean hadn't even needed to use a recipe.

He made everything look so easy.

Since then Dean had seemed to be on some kind of mission. Over the last twenty-four hours he'd been much more attentive to Lucien, spent more time around him, and kept trying to feed him. Lucien wasn't sure what that meant, but it was certainly nice to have someone who cared enough to make him eat better food than microwave meals and toast.

So now, when Dean found Lucien lacing up his boots, Lucien wasn't surprised when he asked him where he was off to.

'I just thought I'd go for a quiet walk to centre myself before the auction.'

Dean paused. 'Can I make you some food to take?'

Lucien couldn't help but smile. 'I won't be gone that long.'

'You want company?'

How to say no without being rude? Lucien couldn't think of a way, and before he knew it Dean had taken advantage of his silence and was pulling on his own boots and grabbing his jacket. He even took a scarf off the hook and looped it over Lucien's shoulders, then reached up to secure it gently around his neck, leaving Lucien flustered and warm.

Lucien's introvert nature meant that being around people drained all his energy—and by God he was going to be around a lot of people later today. He needed to well and truly fill up that well of energy. And that was why he was heading out. There was a place he went to when he needed to recharge.

Dean followed Lucien along the pavement towards the woods at the end of the road, kicking through orange leaves. Lucien kept extra-quiet as he passed the wrought-iron gate that formed the entrance to his grandmother's property. She was often out walking in the grounds, bothering the gardener, and he didn't want her to sense his presence with her ultra-focused grandmother powers like she normally did.

'So, where are we going?' asked Dean loudly, just as they passed her gate.

Lucien sighed and tried hard not to shush him. 'You'll find out when we get there.'

Dean shrugged happily and carried on striding beside Lucien. 'Anyone ever tell you that you walk too fast?'

Lucien slowed his pace slightly. Now that Dean mentioned it, Lucien could hear the man was panting to keep up. Lucien did walk too fast for most people, but it wasn't his fault he had long legs.

They climbed over a stile and walked along the grassy edge of a ploughed field, before taking a left turn and crossing a tiny brook on a short, slippery bridge made from a stone slab covered in moss.

Lucien led the way across an overgrown graveyard towards an old stone church topped with a crooked spire. Every time Lucien came here he was reminded that one day he should come back and tidy the place up. Someone needed to weed around all the headstones, pull the brambles down from the church walls, rake the leaves, perhaps even mow the grass. But, to be honest, he rather liked the ramshackle feel of the place. And the last thing he wanted was for other people to feel welcome there. He liked it hidden—his own overgrown secret. So he'd never quite got around to it.

'Someone should come and neaten this place up,' said Dean, reading Lucien's mind.

Close to the church, the grass was almost crowded out by moss, soft and spongy beneath their boots. Lucien pushed hard on the wooden door of the church until it burst open, its hinges squealing.

'Should we be doing this?' asked Dean. He glanced behind them, as if checking for an angry priest about to yell at them for breaking into his church.

'It's fine—it's deconsecrated. No one uses it any more. In fact, I think I'm the only person who's been here in the last ten years.'

The church had been abandoned years ago. At the time, a handful of people had relocated their loved ones' remains elsewhere, wanting to continue to pay their respects at a place with a priest and a groundskeeper, but most of the graves still held people who'd been gone for hundreds of years. One of the oldest headstones Lucien had seen was for a man named Albie Merrieweather, dated 1699-1728. No one was coming to see him.

Inside it was as quiet as ever. The only noise disrupting the cool, calm air was their echoing footsteps. They walked between the pews to the centre aisle, where stained glass threw red shadows across the wooden floor.

'Now what?' asked Dean.

'We go up.'

Dean followed Lucien to the narrow spiral staircase and they climbed up stone steps built hundreds of years previously. Their middles were worn down and made shiny by centuries of priests' footsteps.

'Be careful, it's pretty uneven.'

Not a moment after Lucien spoke Dean tripped and grabbed the back of Lucien's shirt, cursing quietly as he righted himself.

'I did say…'

'Shut up, Lucien.'

Lucien reached the top, pushed open another stiff wooden door and stepped out on to the bright, breezy tower. He looked out over the chest-high ledge surrounding it and gestured for Dean to join him. The tower was only about ten feet square, and open to the elements, so Lucien's hair was immediately blown into his eyes.

The spire loomed above them, supported by four thick pillars of stone, one on each corner. This left wide spaces on each side of the tower through which to admire the beautiful views.

'Wow, this is a lot higher than I expected.'

Dean stayed in the doorway, biting his lip and holding on with both hands to the doorframe.

Lucien frowned. 'I didn't know you were scared of heights.'

If he'd known he wouldn't have brought him up here.

'I'm not scared, just… How safe is this tower?'

'It's very sturdy. It's been here hundreds of years, and it's made of solid stone.'

Dean peered over the ledge from his place by the door.

'It's safe, I promise,' said Lucien.

Dean reluctantly let go of the doorframe and ventured towards the middle of the platform. Lucien tried not to find it adorable that brave, capable Dean was nervous about being higher than the first floor.

Lucien leaned his arms against the ledge and rested his chin on them. All he could see was green, and it was infinitely calming.

Dean joined him.

'Wow…' Dean turned slowly in place, taking in the three-hundred-and-sixty-degree view. 'I can't see a single building!'

'The trees hide everything,' Lucien answered.

Even though they could see all the way to the horizon in several spots, by coincidence—or somehow by design—all the surrounding villages and farmhouses were hidden from view behind the trees.

He breathed in the smell of woodsmoke and shut his eyes as a cool breeze rustled through trees that would soon overtake the height of the tower. 'I sometimes come here when I get overwhelmed with work. Or family. Or anything.'

'How long have you been coming?'

'Since I was at school. My mother's ashes are scattered here.'

Lucien frowned. He wasn't sure why he had shared that.

Dean stepped closer until their shoulders were touching. 'Where is she?'

Lucien pointed down at one corner of the graveyard, where the grass was lush and thick and covered in a burst of roses and wildflowers in yellow, pink and blue.

Dean nodded. 'Great place to choose.'

'Sometimes I come and talk things over with the flowers when I need help figuring stuff out. It's stupid, but often while I'm here I ask her to give me a sign. You know…that she approves of my decisions.'

Apparently, his mouth could not stop sharing private information with Dean today.

'That's not stupid. What kind of sign?'

Lucien shrugged. 'You can make anything a sign if you want it badly enough. A leaf falling from a tree on to your lap. A bird leaving a feather as it flies away.' Lucien suddenly felt self-conscious. 'Anyway… It's a great place to come and get centred.'

'I can see why you came today, then.' Dean laughed. 'We must be pretty overwhelming.'

Lucien was taken aback. That wasn't why he'd needed to come here at all. In the days since Dean had entered his life not once had he felt the pull to come here because of him and Rafael.

'No. It's not you. It's the auction.'

A wood pigeon fluttered from a tree on to the church roof, and settled down, cooing softly.

'I can see why you like it here,' Dean murmured. 'My blood pressure's lowered already. Could have used a place like this in the city.'

'Where did you go to escape things?'

'I don't know… The gym?'

'You find exercising with a group of strangers relaxing?'

'It felt relaxing in comparison to work, but… Maybe I was kidding myself. To be honest, it feels like coming to Little Champney is the first time I've taken a breath in years.'

'You can come here too if you want. When you need a minute. I don't mind. If you can brave the mountainous heights, that is,' he added as an afterthought.

Dean slapped his arm lightly with the back of his hand. 'Thank you. I just might.' He paused. 'You know, despite being a graveyard, it has quite the romantic vibe.' Dean nudged him playfully with his elbow. 'Do you bring all your dates here?'

Lucien laughed dryly. 'I've never brought anyone here before.'

'Wow. Then I'm touched.'

'You invited yourself, if you remember.'

'Oh, God. I did. Sorry.'

Lucien smiled. 'It's fine. I'm happy to have you.'

It was stimulating to be in Dean's company. And yet he'd found his visit to the church just as relaxing and recharging as he would have had he been alone. The strangeness of that did not escape him.

Dean moved closer, his arm pressing against Lucien's. Lucien tried to suppress the shiver that ran down his spine at the contact. Dean closed his eyes and tilted his face up to the sky, and Lucien took the opportunity to watch how beautifully the breeze caressed Dean's hair and the sun lit his features. His gaze slid slowly down Dean's throat and across his wide, muscular shoulders.

'It's nice being here with you, Lucien,' Dean whispered.

Lucien flinched. While he'd been distracted, Dean had caught him watching. But he didn't seem to mind. In fact, unless Lucien was mistaken, Dean seemed to be rather preoccupied with Lucien's mouth.

Lucien licked his lips briefly and Dean's eyes followed the movement.

Lucien's name sounded wonderful whispered by Dean, and suddenly he couldn't think of anything he wanted more than to hear him say it again.

'Dean?' Lucien murmured, shifting closer.

Dean turned to face him fully. Their fingers collided on the cool stone wall and Lucien held his breath. He swallowed hard, and forced himself not to pull his hand away from Dean's heat. The blood rushed in his ears, and he could barely think straight. Dean moved closer, trailing a hand slowly up Lucien's arm, and he found himself leaning in, drawn like a magnet to Dean's irresistible pull.

A twig cracked loudly in the graveyard below them and they both turned towards the noise. Between the trees, an elderly, very-well-put-together woman appeared, clutching a leather handbag. She smoothly navigated the bridge and mossy grass, despite her sleek high heels.

Lucien stood up straight as soon as he spotted her, and withdrew from Dean. 'Oh, no.'

'What?' asked Dean.

Lucien tried to pull himself together and brushed his clothes off, finding grit from the wall on his sweaty palms. He took a few deep breaths to recover his poise. 'Gird your loins.'

'What? Why are we girding? Who is she?'

The woman looked up at them and saluted. 'Hello, fellas.'

'Hello, Grandmother,' answered Lucien reluctantly.

Dean stared at him for a moment, mouth open, then grinned.

'Who's your young man?' Lucien's grandmother called to them, holding her hand up to shield her eyes from the bright sky.

Lucien rolled his eyes. 'She knows exactly who you are—she just trying to get a reaction. We'll have to go down. But please promise me you'll ignore anything she says. She's an extremely acquired taste.'

They convened between a grave and a small stone angel under the cool shade of an enormous oak tree. Lucien's grandmother looked at him expectantly. And Lucien acquiesced.

'Even though you know perfectly well who he is, let me officially introduce you to Dr Dean Vasquez. Dean, this is Nancy Benedict, my grandmother.'

Dean and Nancy shook hands.

'It's very sweet of you to accompany my grandson here on this difficult day.'

'It is?' asked Dean, looking bewildered.

'Grandmother—' Lucien tried to interrupt.

Nancy touched Lucien's arm briefly. 'I know this day is hard for you, dear.'

Lucien sighed. 'Shall we just go and see her?'

Nancy nodded, and Lucien gestured for her to go first. Then they followed her around the corner of the church towards the wildflower bed.

Lucien spoke quietly as he walked close to Dean. 'It's my mother's birthday today.'

'Oh.' Dean nodded, then looked awkward. 'I'm really sorry I invited myself, man.'

'Don't be. I'm glad you're here.'

Lucien was rewarded with one of Dean's bright smiles, and he nearly stumbled over a tree root.

'Is everything all right?' Lucien asked his

grandmother. 'You don't normally come to see Mother on her birthday.'

Lucien couldn't help but be slightly suspicious that Nancy had appeared so suddenly.

'I remember her in other ways,' Nancy said.

'I know, Grandmother.'

'I mainly came here to find you. Do you have a light, darling?' Nancy pulled a silver cigarette case from her handbag and took out a cigarette.

Lucien rolled his eyes. She knew he always carried a lighter on him, exclusively to light her slim French cigarettes, because she insisted that carrying a lighter of her own was undignified.

'So,' she said, as he held the flame up to light the end of her cigarette. 'I hear you've finally been convinced to join us in the auction?'

'I can always change my mind again,' answered Lucien, feeling himself inching ever closer to doing just that.

Nancy turned to Dean. 'My beloved grandson is not one of life's joiners.'

'Grandmother—'

'No. And we love you despite that…' Nancy spoke over Lucien's protesting '…but every now and again you just have to suck it up. Do you think I enjoy being the chair at every neighbourhood watch and local council meeting?'

'Yes, I do,' answered Lucien.

She paused. 'Well, you're right. But do you really think I enjoy having to attend every church jumble sale and the opening of a new café?'

'Yes. You're usually the one at the centre of any official opening ceremony.'

'It's not my fault I look good with a ribbon and a huge pair of scissors.' Nancy brushed him off. 'Regardless… Can we thank Dean, here, for his good work?' Nancy turned to Dean. 'God knows, I've tried to convince Lucien to take part in the auction for years. But despite decades of my efforts he's refused point blank. Then, strangely, *you* enter the field and he's there in a flash.'

Lucien hoped he could blame his flushed cheeks on the chill in the air.

Dean knocked him gently with his shoulder. 'He'll do a great job, Ms. Benedict. Maybe it's like opening a jar…you loosened the lid and I opened him.'

Lucien's grandmother actually giggled, 'Oh, you are going to be fun. Call me Nancy, please.'

Lucien made a face and looked over at her to check he'd heard correctly. Nancy never giggled. Honestly, Dean needed to be studied by the government—because whatever pheromones he was giving off should be weaponised.

Nancy took Dean's arm as they stood by Lucien's mother's resting place. Since Dean didn't have much of a family himself, he hadn't envisaged bumping into any more of Rafael's. It was blow-ing Dean's mind that Rafael had a great-grandmother—especially as, sadly, his grandmother had already passed. The fact that she was now gripping Dean's arm, only moments after he was pretty sure he'd almost kissed Lucien, was almost too much to handle.

Had he almost kissed Lucien? Or had Lucien almost kissed him? He wasn't sure, but his mind felt scrambled.

After a few moments of silence, when all Dean could hear were the bees bumping lazily from flower to flower and birds singing from the tall trees, Nancy gently cleared her throat.

'I hear you have a young son?'

Dean nodded.

'I must apologise on Lucien's behalf—he has a terrible effect on children.'

'No, Rafael likes Lucien very much.'

Dean glanced over to find Lucien's mouth open and his eyebrows raised, as though Dean had said something surprising.

'And I him,' Lucien said. 'You're both a pleasure to live with.'

It was Nancy's turn to look surprised. She gazed at Lucien for a moment, before addressing Dean. 'He must be a very special child.'

'Thank you—he is.'

'It's so nice of you to provide your family with a child to dote upon. They must be so happy to have him.' She looked back pointedly at Lucien.

Dean rubbed the back of his neck. He hadn't signed up for this. Keeping the truth from Lucien was bad enough, but now he was lying to one more of Rafael's blood relatives, and neither of them knew about it but him. It reminded Dean how closely he was flirting with danger. There was so much riding on this situation that he'd got them all into. And if it all went wrong there were so many people who would be affected.

'I'm not in contact with most of my family,' he said. Which was why it would mean so much if these people welcomed Rafael into theirs.

Dean tried to imagine Nancy interacting with Rafael. He wasn't sure she was the type to bake him cookies or knit him a winter hat…

'Oh. I'm sorry, dear. You know, I've always found Little Champney to be very welcoming to people in need of a new start.' Nancy patted Dean's arm, then briefly squeezed his hand before letting go.

Dean felt a burst of affection. She might not be a bad great-grandmother at all.

Which was why he could never risk a relationship with Lucien.

Dean's heart plummeted at the realisation.

Lying to Lucien was so much harder than he'd expected it to be. And when Dean finally told Lucien his secret there was no knowing how Lucien would react. Dean still believed in his reasons for hiding the truth—Rafael had to come first. But that was exactly why Dean must never complicate things by falling for Lucien. If things went wrong…if they ended badly… Dean would be forced to rip Rafael away from the only blood family he had.

Thank God Dean hadn't kissed Lucien.

He had narrowly avoided a complete disaster, and he couldn't risk doing the same thing again.

All the Zen Lucien had built up at his beloved tumbledown church was obliterated as he and Dean approached the town hall together.

They passed the bouncy castle on the green, and stopped for a minute to wave hello to Helen and Rafael. Dean grabbed Rafael and gave him a quick hug, before sending him back to the castle, and then they made their way towards the town hall entrance.

Lucien had kept so far away from this event for the last decade that he hadn't even seen the hall decorated for it before. When he'd last attended they'd never bothered to decorate the outside. But today there were countless banners of brightly coloured fabric—probably handmade by the Women's Institute—and the trees on the cobblestone forecourt were strung with warm white fairy lights. He hadn't known it was possible for a building to be covered in quite that much bunting…

'Looks like Christmas,' said Dean.

Lucien was too nervous to speak, and just grunted in reply. Then he saw something truly horrendous, and stopped walking just outside the entrance. Dean bumped hard into his back, but it didn't move Lucien one inch. Before Dean could say anything, Lucien grabbed his arm and pointed at the door with his other hand.

When Dean saw what he was pointing at he burst out laughing, but Lucien did not see the funny side. Covering one half of the door was a large poster advertising the auction. Underneath the time and day of the event was a list of the people who would be going up for auction. And right in the middle, clear as day, in jaunty purple Comic Sans lettering, were the words *Sexy GPs Dr Lucien Benedict and Dr Dean Vasquez!*

'"Sexy GPs"?' Lucien eventually spluttered out.

When Dean finally took a look at Lucien's face he grimaced sympathetically. 'They're just having a bit of fun, I'm sure they don't mean anything bad by it.'

Lucien massaged his temples with both hands, feeling the beginnings of a headache. 'I trained as a doctor for ten years—how has it resulted in this? We both did. Doesn't this bother you?'

Dean shrugged. 'The use of Comic Sans does.' He rubbed Lucien's arm and glanced back at the poster. 'It's okay. It'll be okay. Look—they've called the vicar "handsome".'

Lucien checked. They had.

'And they've called Mayor Jean "enchanting".'

Lucien nodded, feeling his heart rate come down slowly. He was not sure if it was Dean's words, or the fact that he was still rubbing Lucien's arm comfortingly.

'We can do this.' Dean made eye contact with Lucien, and smiled. 'Or, if you really don't want to, we can go back home right now.'

They stared at each other for a long moment. Dean's eyes really were a wonderful shade of green…

'Lucien?'

Oh. Yes. 'Let's go in and get this over with.'

Dean winked, patted his arm once more, and they walked inside.

They crossed the small reception area and peeked into the hall. The room was cavernous, and brimming with people on his grandmother's organisational team. The stage at the far end made Lucien feel sick with nerves when he looked at it. There were maybe two hundred chairs set up in rows, pointed at the stage, and behind those sat a large wooden dance floor, with speakers and DJ equipment set up in one corner. To the side of that was a dining area, with several circular tables covered with white tablecloths, and long tables laden with buffet food.

The hall was often used for big weddings, plays and dances, and it had plenty of room for everything. High windows cast shafts of bright light on to the chaos beneath. Two people were on tall ladders, still stringing the last few lengths of bunting, and others rushed around beneath them, getting the chairs into neater lines and adding cutlery to tables. The doors were due to open to the public in half an hour, so anything they didn't get done soon would have to go undone.

Still hesitating at the entrance, Lucien and Dean were grabbed by Betty, Nancy's personal assistant—a woman Lucien had known his whole life. She dragged them through the hall to a back room, surprisingly strong for someone so small, and Lucien wouldn't have been surprised if her tiny hand had left a bruise after gripping his forearm so tightly.

'Dean—meet Betty,' he forced out through gritted teeth.

Dean laughed. 'Lovely to meet you.'

Betty hadn't yet said a word to either of them. She pushed them up a narrow, creaking staircase and deposited them both on a threadbare old couch by a window.

'This is the green room. You have half an hour before the auction starts. Do *not* go missing.' She punctuated her order by pointing directly at Lucien.

'I'll keep my eye on him, Betty,' said Dean.

Betty gave a rare warm smile. 'I'm sure you will, dear.'

And with that she was gone, in a whirlwind of pleated skirt and lavender.

'How come she likes *you*?' Lucien asked. 'You've only known her thirty seconds—she's known me thirty years.'

'Just my natural charm, I guess.'

There were already two other people in the green room, chatting in the corner by a decrepit-looking coffee machine—probably another two victims for the auction. One looked vaguely familiar, but Lucien couldn't quite muster up the concentration to place him.

'How are you holding up?' asked Dean.

And with that, Lucien's nerves came rushing back.

He stood up. 'I'm fine. Stop fussing.'

If he didn't talk about it he could pretend it wasn't happening—at least for a while. He leaned his forehead on the cool glass of the window. There were already small groups of people on the forecourt, waiting for the doors to open. Panic flooded his chest and he took a deep breath.

Maybe making an awful cup of coffee would take his mind off things.

Lucien left Dean over by the window and grabbed two paper cups from a stack behind the coffee machine.

'I wouldn't drink that, if I were you.'

Lucien looked up to find the friendly brown

eyes and messy blond hair of the village vet, Nika. So that was who the vaguely familiar man was.

'You're not being sold off too?' asked Lucien.

'Your grandmother's a very persuasive woman.'

'Tell me about it…'

'I noticed you and your fellow "sexy GP" advertised outside.'

Lucien's face grew warm again, and he glanced back at Dean, who smiled, openly listening to their conversation.

'Sadly I didn't make it on to the poster,' Nika continued. 'But I like to think my descriptor would have been "adorable local vet".'

Nika and Lucien had been out for dinner once, about five years ago. Nika had asked him out, and Lucien hadn't been able to figure out a polite way to decline, so had found himself saying yes to avoid the awkwardness of the moment. The evening had been typically disastrous, and they'd turned out to share not a hint of sexual chemistry, despite how handsome and charismatic Nika clearly was.

'Well, it certainly wouldn't be modest,' Lucien replied.

Nika laughed good-naturedly. 'I can't believe you're doing this. I didn't think it was your sort of thing. You know there'll be hundreds of people watching?'

Suddenly the enormity of what he was about to do hit Lucien all over again, and he found it hard to catch his breath. He fumbled with the paper cups, but before he knew it a strong hand had taken his shoulder and gently led him back over to the sofa by the window.

Dean pushed him on to the seat, then knelt on the floor in front of him.

Nika grimaced an apology, then backed off and resumed his previous conversation.

When Lucien was sure they'd both stopped watching him, he was able to tune in to what Dean was saying.

'Lucien? Look at me.'

Dean spoke quietly and calmly. And when he told Lucien to breathe, Lucien did. Big, deep, calming breaths, just like Dean said. He focused on Dean's face, his eyes glowing green in the golden hour light from the window, his jawline strong and faintly stubbled. This close, he could see the flecks of brown in just one eye, and the freckles scattered adorably over his nose.

Lucien felt guilty for putting that worried look on his beautiful face.

'Are you okay?' asked Dean.

Lucien wanted to say yes. He wasn't used to being open about his anxieties. His life had been full of bad experiences when people had made him feel foolish for sharing them.

In the past, when he'd felt nervous about doing something, the people closest to him had either forced him to do it, or suggested he was being lazy or stupid and tried to shame him into doing it. He knew by now that it came from a place of love, however misguided and ignorant, at least where his grandmother was concerned. And he had ended up as a successful doctor, hadn't he? So his grandmother was convinced she'd helped his mother raise him the right way. As if any success he'd found was down to her, rather than despite her.

She would never change. But he knew she truly loved him and meant well. She was simply from a different time. He'd learned to humour her and not take what she said to heart.

But, either way, he'd learned to hide his anxieties from other people. No one wanted their doctor to show vulnerability. He had become excellent at pretending and masking and covering when he needed to. He wasn't stupid enough to think that was the healthiest way to deal with his anxiety, but it was all he could do right now. Maybe when he retired, in thirty years, he'd have time to find a therapist and become happy and well adjusted.

'Lucien?' Dean said, and Lucien got the feeling Dean might have said his name more than once. 'Are you okay?'

Lucien nodded and tried to carry off a casual smile, brushing the whole thing off. But the way Dean rubbed one thumb over his shoulder so gently made his smile wobble and he gave up trying to pretend.

'Dean, I don't think I can do this. I can't wait here for my name to be announced and then parade across the stage with everyone looking at me. I just can't.'

Dean stared at him for a second. 'Is that the part you're most scared of?'

Lucien frowned. He didn't quite understand why he was being asked that question, but he thought about it anyway. 'Yes, I think so.'

'Wait here. I'll be back in a minute.'

Dean left.

Suddenly alone, Lucien leaned his head back against the cool wall and tried to continue the deep breathing. He wiped the sweat from his temples and upper lip on his sleeve, then spent the next few minutes battling with the ancient window, trying to open it enough to let a bit of air in.

Dean returned five minutes later, red-faced and breathing heavily, his shirt untucked.

'What on earth have you been up to?'

'I've sorted it. Betty wasn't happy with me at first, but I asked her to change a few things last minute. When the curtain comes up all the auctionees will already be seated onstage behind a line of tables. The MC will stand by each of us in turn to auction us off. No big entrance. You'll just have to sit there. And a table will be in between you and the audience. How's that?'

Lucien was amazed by how much better he felt. The relief washed over him, and he took his first easy breath in what felt like ages. Then he took another look at Dean, trying to tuck his shirt back in and straighten himself up using the window as a makeshift mirror.

'Thank you, Dean.'

Dean shrugged his gratitude off. 'I'm here to serve.'

'I mean it. But I have to ask… How did you become so unkempt in the space of five minutes?'

'I had to move all the tables.'

Lucien laughed. 'I'm sorry.'

'Why?'

'I'm sorry I'm like this.'

Dean looked puzzled. 'Like what?'

Lucien shrugged. 'Making a fuss about nothing.'

'It's not nothing if it makes you anxious.'

Lucien shook his head. Dean didn't understand. 'I'm a grown man. I shouldn't mind being in front of a crowd. And it's not just here. I didn't exactly pull my weight at the school event either. I'm sorry I left you to do all the work.'

Dean shook his head. 'Don't say that. Different people have different strengths, and it's okay to play to them. I love doing the talking, so you don't have to.'

'Then what do *I* bring to the table?'

'You look pretty!' Dean joked.

That surprised a laugh out of Lucien.

'You connected with those kids one on one,'

Dean continued. 'They loved you. Stop worrying about it. You're exactly who you're supposed to be. Our differences make us work better as a team. Think of the chaos if everyone loved being the centre of attention. Two of me would be a nightmare.'

'That's true,' Lucien said, lying through his teeth.

To him, two Deans sounded amazing.

Dean was the first person he'd ever known who didn't want him to put on a mask. Dean never made him feel small. He listened to his worries, then found a way he could help him. It was what Lucien had always wanted but hadn't thought was possible, or maybe deserved. He was used to doing everything the hard way. Now he had a friend who would help him… It seemed unlikely, but okay…

'Thanks for helping me,' he said.

'It's nothing—forget it.'

Lucien nodded, and almost did as Dean asked. But something welled up in his chest and he started talking without even meaning to.

'It's not nothing. Everyone's always told me I'm too quiet, or too introverted. It's made me feel like my personality is wrong, somehow. That I'd be a better person if I would just be more extroverted. It started in school and it'd carried on through college, university, the workplace. *Join in more...speak up more...socialise more...date more*... Their demands may come from a well-meaning place, but it's relentless. And, as much as I try to block it out, sometimes it still hurts.' He paused. 'As sad as it might seem, you're the first person who seems to accept me as I am.'

Dean looked embarrassed as hell by Lucien's little speech. He scratched at a loose thread on the sofa between them and stared down at his hand.

'Of course I accept you, man. You're awesome. All I want to do is try to help make the difficult things easier for you. You deserve to have someone around who can do that.'

Lucien didn't know what to say.

Betty chose that moment to march them backstage. Two doctors, along with a vicar, a vet and a mayor. The thought that it sounded like the set-up for a joke flashed through Lucien's mind in a moment of deranged panic.

As they stood quietly in the wings Dean slung an arm over Lucien's shoulder and squeezed him tight for a second. Lucien hoped Dean couldn't feel him shaking. Whether that was nerves, or surprise at being suddenly crushed into Dean's warm, hard chest, he wasn't entirely sure.

'We're gonna be fine,' whispered Dean, directly into Lucien's ear, just for him to hear.

And, God help him, Lucien almost believed it.

Dean clearly couldn't wait for his time in the limelight. His eyes were bright and excited, and it seemed he couldn't wipe the grin off his face.

Lucien marvelled over Dean's enthusiasm. 'You're actually looking forward to being out there, aren't you?'

'You can't keep a good show-off down.'

Never had Lucien felt more that he and Dean were two different species. But Dean looked beautiful like this. Confident, excited, happy. He was truly in his element. If they weren't surrounded by people he might be tempted to take a second try at that almost-kiss they hadn't talked about…

The curtain still down, Betty dragged Lucien and Dean by their elbows to two seats behind the long row of tables Dean must have moved earlier. The tables were now covered in plain white tablecloths and had name cards by each chair. Lucien's knee jigged up and down as he wiped his palms on his trousers and tried to find a way to sit comfortably in the wooden chair. The legs screeched on the stage as he moved it closer to Dean.

'Stop fidgeting!' Betty whispered furiously.

The crowd on the other side of the curtain were invisible, but audible. A constant hum of chatter, laughs and coughs. Lucien thought his heart might beat out of his chest—until he felt a nudge in his side. He turned to find Dean smiling at him. He winked, and Lucien calmed down slightly.

'You good?' Dean whispered.

'I still don't like the thought of having all that attention on me, but I can do this.'

'Don't worry. I'll make sure their attention is elsewhere.'

As the curtain swept back to reveal the cheering hordes Lucien just had time to fully regret his life choices before his heart started racing at such a speed he genuinely started to calculate how long it would take an ambulance to travel from the hospital to get here and treat him for a stroke. But then Dean squeezed his knee under the table with one large hand, and Lucien took a breath. He noticed that everyone in the audience was smiling and clapping. He wasn't dying…he was okay.

The evening's MC was enthusiasm personified, and while his manner made Lucien cringe a little, he was actually very good at his job, and had the audience whipped into an excitable frenzy within minutes. He announced each of their names in turn, with the crowd going increasingly crazy with each one.

When he got to Dean, Dean jumped up on to his chair and extended his arms, playing to the audience and whipping them up even more. Half the WI screamed as if they were at a rock concert.

And when the MC announced Lucien's name next, he felt secure in the knowledge that not a single soul in that hall was looking at him.

Dean gazed down from his chair and grinned at Lucien.

Except one, perhaps. And it felt wonderful.

The MC continued with his patter, explaining

each of the prizes. Lucien had settled on giving a two-hour climbing lesson on the climbing wall in the nearest large town. While Dean had kept it simple, just offering to go out to dinner with the highest bidder. The MC somehow managed to make each offer sound exciting, and had the crowd responding enthusiastically to all of them. Nika the vet's prize was him painting a portrait of the winner's pet, and the mayor's was a tour of the council buildings and trying on the mayor's robe and chains.

Which didn't sound like much compared to a date with Dean, if Lucien was honest.

'Are you sure about this date thing?' Lucien murmured to Dean from the corner of his mouth.

'I don't have any hidden talents in art or climbing mountains. In fact I have no skills to offer the Little Champney public at all other than being a thoroughly charming date.'

Lucien laughed. He almost found himself relaxing—until the bidding started.

Dean was second up, and he stood as his name was announced. He did a slow, confident spin, displaying himself for the audience and making them laugh.

'I'll start us off at fifty pounds,' the MC said into his microphone.

About six different hands went up and the crowd tittered. Within what seemed like seconds, and after much shouting and catcalling, they were up to five hundred pounds.

Lucien smiled at how keen everyone was—and quite rightly too. He craned his neck to see who was bidding so high on Dean. But the stage lights shone into his eyes and made him squint. He had assumed some nice, retired lady might bid on Dean and take him for afternoon tea, but from what little he could hear and see there was actually a furious bidding war taking place between various men and women way too young and attractive for Lucien's liking.

Dean was clearly being spurred on by the crowd's energy. He jumped up and punched the air when his total was declared at six hundred and fifty pounds, and waved at the winner before sitting back down. Lucien couldn't help but laugh at Dean's smug look.

But then it was Lucien's turn to be bid on. He exhaled heavily and made sure not to make eye contact with anybody. If he steeled himself, this would all be over soon. No one would bid on him, it would be humiliating, and then it would be over.

He was shocked and flattered to find that he received what might almost be considered a flurry of bids. Again, he couldn't see who was bidding, but the MC ended Lucien's auction on a total only just less than Dean's. Evidently someone out there really wanted to learn how to climb…

The rest of the auction seemed to fly by in

seconds, and before Lucien knew it they were climbing down from the stage. He felt light as a feather, and even a little drunk, although he hadn't touched a drop of alcohol.

Dean nudged him as they reached the bottom step. 'You did great!'

'Thank you! I think I'm experiencing some kind of adrenaline high.'

'That'll do it.'

Villagers came at him from all sides, with smiles and handshakes and congratulations—as if he'd just got married or won the lottery.

'They're just happy to see you here,' said Dean, in response to his quizzical look.

Lucien hadn't felt this good in years. He even felt the stirrings of an unfamiliar emotion. If he wasn't mistaken, he was actually feeling quite proud of himself for having taken the leap. It hadn't been as horrific as he'd feared, but without Dean's help he never would have found that out.

'Best auction in years, Dr Benedict.'

A patient he knew from the clinic took his hand and shook it vehemently. When Lucien finally got his hand back he thanked her, and moved on to the next waiting congratulator.

Everyone was being so nice. He knew it was Dean's charismatic contribution that had made it the best auction in years, but he was quite pleased to have been a part of it nonetheless. It was nice to feel so much goodwill poured his way. Maybe he was more liked than he'd thought. Maybe he was a part of the village too—not just a useful cog people tolerated because of his mother and his grandmother.

He certainly wasn't going to become some social butterfly, but maybe once in a while it would be safe to step out of his box…just for a second. Dean had come to Little Champney and everything had changed. Lucien's life was busier, the village was brighter, and the practice was more involved with the community. People Lucien had kept at a safe distance for the last decade were suddenly becoming a part of his life.

Helen appeared, carrying Rafael on her hip, even though he was really getting too big to be held. One of her teenage daughters walked alongside and fed him sweets one by one, straight out of the packet.

'You were both amazing!' said Helen. 'I would have bid, but I had my eye on the vet.'

Dean grabbed Rafael's face and kissed him loudly, ignoring his mortified squirming. 'I see you're being well served by your minions.'

'He's been such a good boy.'

'Did you see us on stage, Raf?'

Rafael nodded. 'Helen gave me a chocolate cupcake.'

'Fair enough—that *is* the bigger news of the evening,' answered Dean.

They mingled a little longer, then Nancy pulled

Lucien away to introduce him to some local councillors she'd been trying to get him to meet for years. Lucien soon found himself close to reaching the maximum on his social meter. He'd just had time to wonder where Dean had got to, when the man himself appeared at Lucien's shoulder.

'There you are!' said Dean. 'Have you met your winner yet?'

'She's gone home already. Apparently she wanted the session for her teenage son.'

A beautiful woman appeared at Dean's side.

'Oh, this is Jenny—my winner.' Dean stepped back to give her some room. 'We're heading out now.'

'You are?' said Lucien.

'On our date,' she trilled, flashing her teeth and snaking a hand over Dean's forearm.

'No time like the present.' Dean smiled at Lucien and shrugged. 'Helen suggested we do it this evening. She offered—actually, more like begged—to look after Raf overnight for me. I've already run back home and packed him an overnight bag. So that means you can stay out…or go home and make the most of the peace and quiet.'

Lucien nodded. Jenny was very pretty. He could see why Dean would jump at the chance to spend the evening with her.

Dean punched Lucien's arm lightly. 'See you at home?'

Lucien nodded as Dean and Jenny made their

way across the emptying dance floor. Peace and quiet sounded very good right now. But Lucien stayed where he was, hovering by the food tables, feeling strangely empty.

Next to the buffet was always a good place to stand if you wanted to avoid conversation by looking busy, and it also offered the added bonus of having something to do with your hands, so you didn't look like a spare part. He selected a breadstick that looked as if it probably hadn't been grabbed by the grubby hands of children, and nibbled on it as he watched Dean and Jenny leave the building, her arm still wrapped around his like a limpet.

A moment later, he watched Helen take Rafael home. He smiled fondly as Rafael grabbed her hand before stepping outdoors, just as Dean always told him to. Then, realising everyone he really cared to speak to had left, Lucien decided to go home too. His ordeal was over! He was free to escape, and escape he would. He had things to do at home, and this was the perfect chance to take advantage of an empty house.

'I'm so glad I won. Tessa from the bakery put up quite a fight, but I knew I could come out on top. She beat me last year when I bid for a date with the dentist. Have you met him yet? He's very good-looking, but he obviously didn't like Tessa at all. She ended up settling for her old school boyfriend…they're married now. If it had been me, I wouldn't have let a dentist slip through my fingers. I love a man in uniform, you know?'

Dean hadn't yet got a word in edgeways, and was swiftly regretting ever taking part in the auction at all. But at least he could get this date with Jenny over and done with in one night.

How early would it not be rude to leave?

'I'm a bit disappointed you're not wearing your white coat and stethoscope, actually.'

Dean laughed, but then slowly realised she wasn't joking.

'Can't really wear them out of the surgery. Anyway, don't you like what I'm wearing now?' he asked, mock insulted.

'Oh, yes.' She looked him up and down longingly. 'You look gorgeous. So, where are you taking me on our romantic date?'

'Uh… I just thought we'd grab a quick meal at the Horse and Hare?'

'Oh, okay.'

She looked disappointed for a moment. Then shrugged and shoved her arm through his as they walked.

Helen had told Dean that it was a nice place to eat. He hadn't wanted somewhere romantic, as he'd assumed the person who won wouldn't be treating it like an actual date—rather as a fun chat and an interesting way to donate to the charity. At least the food was supposed to be great there. He wanted to get something enjoyable out of the evening.

Dean racked his brain for something to say that wouldn't result in her flirting with him again. 'So, what do you do for a living, Jenny?'

'I love the way you say my name. Such a sexy accent.'

Dean tried subtly to pull his arm from her grip, but she just tightened her hold and he gave up.

'I don't think I really have an interesting accent…it's just London.'

'I wish I lived in London. It must be so exciting there.'

'Have you ever been?'

'Only once. We went on a school trip to see a musical in one of the theatres in the West End. I bet you went to the theatre every weekend when you lived there.'

'Oh, God no. I'm not that into plays. And certainly not musicals.'

'I love them. *Mamma Mia* is my favourite. Don't you just love Abba?'

Dean did not, but he hummed vaguely in response.

'Oh, silly me—I didn't answer your question! I'm a hairdresser.'

She reached out, and before Dean could even blink she'd run a cold hand through his hair.

'Looks like you need a cut and style.' She magicked up a business card as if from nowhere and thrust it at him. 'Promise me you'll come to me soon?'

Dean took the card and grunted as noncommittally as he could. 'Curl Up and Dye,' he read out. 'Nice pun.'

'Thank you! I came up with it myself. I'm so glad you like it.' She paused. 'So, the most important question of the evening...'

Dean dreaded to think what that was going to be.

'Do you have a girlfriend? Or a wife, even?'

'No, I don't.'

Lucien's face suddenly popped into his mind for some reason. He wondered how he was doing at the auction, and if he'd left to go home yet.

'I heard you have a son?'

Dean tuned back in to the conversation. 'Yes, that's true.'

Jenny proceeded to gush about how great she was with kids and how she'd love to meet him. But Dean was not getting good vibes from her. He was getting *I want to spend time with you because you're a doctor who wears a white coat and I'll say anything to make you like me* vibes. She might be a very nice person, if she ever got real for one minute and stopped saying whatever she thought would impress him the most.

A plump pigeon landed on the pavement in front of them, chasing a stray chip. Jenny let out a little scream and kicked out her foot in its general direction. 'Horrible creatures,' she said with a shiver.

Then again, he might be giving her a little too much credit.

She might be some people's perfect cup of tea. But she certainly wasn't Dean's.

He yanked open the door to the pub, and warm air and the smell of food smacked him in the face. He ushered her through with a flourish, wanting to get the evening over and done with.

After a couple of hours of polite but uninspiring conversation, Dean was thoroughly losing the will to live. He'd drunk two or three halves of bitter, by that point, and eaten one plate of chips and a delicious burger to soak it up, and now he was running out of things to talk about.

'So, what did you do today at work?' asked Jenny. 'Your job must be so exciting.'

Dean thought back to the abscess he'd drained in the morning, and the intimate rash he'd inspected last thing. 'I can't really discuss any patient details.'

'Oh, please… There must be something you can tell me?'

Dean took a long sip of his drink, and wondered again how early he could politely bail on this date. 'It was all very mundane, I promise.'

The only exciting moment of the day had been when Lucien had spilled lukewarm coffee all over himself and decided to change his shirt right in the middle of the staff room. As if that was a perfectly normal thing to do and wouldn't give any innocent passing colleagues heart palpitations.

But she probably didn't want to hear about that—and Dean didn't want to share it. That was a memory just for him.

'What are you smiling at?' she asked.

'Nothing.' He drained his glass.

Despite all the facts, Jenny obviously saw this as a real date, and Dean knew it was time to end the evening and stop wasting her time.

She'd find the right one eventually. But would Dean?

'It's getting late. I should see you home.'

Dean stood and passed Jenny her coat, then shrugged on his own.

'No need. I live literally two doors away. But how sweet! You're such a romantic. I knew you would be.'

Dean attempted a smile that he was sure turned out as more of a grimace. He held out his hand to shake hers, and she took it after a short hesitation.

'It was lovely to make a new friend,' he said.

She nodded, smiling. 'Message received.'

Dean was taken aback. He hadn't expected her to give up the chase so easily. Maybe they actually could be friends.

Dean sighed, feeling relaxed for the first time that evening. Finally he could get back to Lucien.

Ever since he'd found Lucien trying his hardest to make Rafael pancakes, even though he'd had no clue how, simply because Rafael had asked him to, something had shifted in his heart. Something had clicked into place and he wanted to be around Lucien all the time. He felt this strange need to take care of him, protect him—something he'd never felt before outside of his family. He wished Lucien were here with him now. He would have loved that burger…

Would kissing Lucien really be that much of a risk? What if things between them ended well? Wouldn't it be worth it?

Maybe Helen was right.

Maybe Dean had found the right one already.

CHAPTER SIX

LUCIEN WAS ALONE for what felt like the first time in weeks, and it was the perfect moment to finally finish the project he'd been working on.

Lucien pulled on an old sweatshirt and went to the garage, to grab a few bits and pieces from the cupboard behind his car. He hummed industriously as he carried them to the kitchen floor and sorted through them, evidently still coasting on a high from the auction, mixed with a huge dose of relief that it was over.

He was still in disbelief that he'd tried something that terrified him and that it had gone well. It probably would have been a disaster without Dean. But Lucien liked to think he might have had something to do with it himself too. He'd had a shot of self-confidence, and it was a hell of a drug.

He smiled and twirled a paintbrush in his hand, feeling quite pleased with himself.

His mood wasn't perfect, though. He couldn't say he was completely happy that Dean was out on his date. The woman had seemed altogether too interested in him for Lucien's liking. He'd only seen them together for a minute, but in that one minute she had touched Dean six times. Not that Lucien had been counting. And not that he was feeling territorial over his house mate. Dean could date whomever he wanted. He could go on dates every night of the week if that was what he was into.

Lucien took a breath.

She was just an auction winner. And it was none of his business anyway. Plus, he had other things to think about. He smiled as he gathered up a small tin of blue paint and a paint-spattered plastic tray and roller, then trotted upstairs with his arms full to the first floor.

He flung open the door to his office and deposited his things on the carpet, then looked around at the almost empty room. He'd been planning this for a week now, and there wasn't all that much left to do. He'd already sneaked a lot of his office equipment into his bedroom, while Dean had been working or out with Rafael. He'd been surprised to find there was plenty of room under his bedroom window to put his desk and chair. It would be perfectly fine to have a bedroom office. He'd also managed to move out all his books and boxes of files without anyone noticing.

He'd bought the paint from the independent hardware store near the surgery after asking Rafael what his favourite colour was—subtly, he hoped. He was only planning to paint one wall as an accent. The cream walls had only been repainted last year, and they were still in perfect shape—plus they were half covered in built-in shelves anyway. Which meant Rafael would have plenty of room for all his toys and books.

He spread out a plastic sheet over the carpet and popped open the paint tin with a screwdriver. When he realised he hadn't brought up a stick to stir the paint with, he shrugged and used the screwdriver. As long as he remembered to rinse it off before it dried it wouldn't be too much of a disaster. He didn't have time to keep running up and down stairs. He wanted this done before Dean got home from his date. And there was no knowing when that might be.

Part of him hoped Dean was having a terrible time with Miss Grabby Hands, and that he escaped to come home early, but the other part of him needed him to be out for a couple more hours so he could get this finished.

He painted all the edges carefully with a paintbrush, and had the first coat rolled on and finished within thirty minutes. He rinsed off the screwdriver in the kitchen sink, washed out the roller, and made himself a coffee to keep his energy up. Then he started doing everything else.

He took down his thick charcoal-coloured curtains, and put up some blue ones with rocket ships on, then unrolled a small matching rug.

The biggest job left to do was building the flat-pack bunk bed he'd purchased, but he'd already managed to pre-make it into two pieces, and it was stashed in the unused shed in the garden. It had been locked in there for two days, since he'd popped back for a couple of lunch breaks to put it together. It had been worth going back to work a bit sweaty and out of breath. Although it had caused a few jokes at work about what on earth he'd been up to.

Dean seemed like the kind of guy who could build a bed from scratch with his own two hands, so he'd worked hard on making the bunk bed look at least passable.

Lucien jogged down to the shed and grabbed the first piece. It was pretty light, being for a small child, and he manoeuvred it up the stairs with no problem. When he came back for the second piece he had to have a little break while he caught his breath. He might have overestimated his fitness level… After a few deep breaths, he grabbed the second piece, locked the shed door, and hefted it up the stairs a little more slowly than the first one.

All the bed needed was a few extra screws drilled in to attach the two halves together. Once it was sturdy and safe, he grabbed the two little mattresses from where they'd been hidden under his own bed and the bunk bed was finished. It would need Rafael's quilt and pillow, but he'd let Dean and Rafael add those. He didn't feel comfortable going into their room by himself.

After all that, he touched the paint on the wall with his fingertips. Dry enough for the second coat.

When he'd finally finished painting, and cleaned up Rafael's new room as much as he could, he pulled on the bathroom light and looked in the mirror. What he saw made him tut in annoyance, and he wet a cloth, then tried to wipe off the dozens of tiny blue dots he'd spattered all over his face.

He checked the time. Eight o'clock. Dean and that woman had been having dinner for maybe two hours by now. So he must be having a decent time, then. Lucien tried to ignore the drop in his stomach that thought aroused. Dean was probably just being polite. She had bid a lot for the date, after all. It would be rude not to give her a decent chunk of time and a nice meal.

What would a date with Dean be like? He was ridiculously charming and harmlessly flirty with everyone at the best of times. Date Dean must be ten times more attractive and intimate and attentive. He'd probably pull the chair out for her at the table. Compliment her on her clothes. Listen to her closely as if she was the only person on Earth.

She was probably halfway in love with him

by now, Lucien thought glumly. And he couldn't blame her. Who could resist Date Dean?

The house was so quiet without Dean and Rafael. Even when Dean returned it would still feel strange to be alone together, just the two of them, with no Rafael running around. When Dean got back, would they sit together? Would Dean tell him all about the date? Would Lucien be able to talk about Dean's night like a grown man without sounding like a jealous idiot?

It was a shame nothing could ever happen between them…almost a waste of an empty house.

Lucien shook his head. He was being ridiculous.

The only thing left to do to Rafael's room was add the final finishing touch. He'd seen an embarrassingly large blue gift bow in the shop in town, and at the time he'd thought it might be a nice idea to stick it on the door of Rafael's new bedroom. But now he was looking at it in the stark light of home he felt like an idiot.

This wasn't him. He wasn't demonstrative. It was just a stupid piece of decorative ribbon.

But somehow it seemed to mean more than that. Much more.

Ugh, this was mortifying.

He ripped the backing off the ribbon and slammed it on to the outside of the door, then stalked off before he could change his mind.

At nine o'clock Dean still wasn't back.

Lucien had put all his painting equipment and tools back in the garage. He'd hoovered the carpet after he'd noticed some sawdust from drilling the bunk bed. He'd slightly rearranged everything in the bedroom, drawn the curtains, brought up a lamp from the living room to make the room feel cosier, and left it on, so that when Dean saw the room it would look its best. He'd even grabbed a few of Rafael's toys that were lying around the kitchen and sofa and brought them up to arrange on the empty shelves, to make it look a bit more like a kid's room.

He'd finally decided there wasn't anything else he could do, and he was now just fiddling, so he closed the door, adjusted the bow, considered for the tenth time taking it off and throwing it in the bin, decided not to, and then left it alone.

His body ached from all the traipsing up and down stairs, but he was too hyped up to rest. He tried reading a book, but attempted to read the same paragraph fifteen times before he gave up in frustration. He sighed and grabbed the TV remote. There must be something he could watch.

At ten o'clock, with still not a hint of Dean, he suddenly had a horrible thought. What if Dean didn't come home at all? What if he'd had such a great time that they'd decided to have drinks after the meal, and then they'd kissed, and then Dean had gone to her house for the night?

The more he sat with that thought, the more

likely it seemed. They were both adults, they were both confident, probably sexually active single people, he assumed. Otherwise why would she have bid for a date with Dean?

Of course they were going to sleep together. That was what normal people did. Just because Lucien had become a person who couldn't even consider sleeping with someone unless he'd known them for months and felt completely comfortable with them, it didn't mean that most people felt that way. A lot of people were perfectly comfortable sleeping with someone they'd just met. And, as long as everything was consensual and safe, there was absolutely nothing wrong with that.

Lucien just wasn't built that way. At least not any more. The only time he'd ever been with someone he hadn't had serious feelings for was when he'd slept with that girl at medical school. What was her name? Cheryl…? Carla…? Charlie. That was it.

She'd been an amazing friend. But he'd known perfectly well he wasn't attracted to her—not in any real way. She'd been beautiful, and funny, and a way cooler person than he'd had any right to be friends with. But she'd been the kind of person who was kind to everybody—even the biggest dork at medical school. Which was how Lucien had thought of himself, despite how many people told him he was wrong.

They'd only slept together because they'd both been drunk and silly and it had been the last day of university. She'd said she wanted to do something that she'd never done before. One last social experiment before she left university and had to be a proper adult. And, as she was mostly attracted to women, sleeping with a man was one thing she'd never done before. Lucien had found himself perfectly happy to oblige. Drinking had always made him a little horny, and very bad at decision-making.

The next morning he'd expected to regret it, but it had been the perfect morning-after. She'd made him banana pancakes, he'd made her a caramel iced coffee—from a packet—and then they'd bade each other farewell for ever, smiling, happy and perfectly at ease with their silly, rebellious last night as students. They'd promised to keep in touch, but he'd known they probably wouldn't. Like so many other people he'd felt close to in medical school, they were all too soon consumed with their own lives.

Lucien sank down further on to the sofa and swung his legs up onto the cushions. He reached behind him to the shelf that held his alcohol collection and tumbler glasses. This had suddenly turned into an evening that required whisky.

Of course Dean wasn't coming home. The date had gone well, and Dean, for one rare night, was free from any responsibility. Maybe even free for the first time since he'd had Rafael. Of course he was going to stay over and spend the night with a beautiful, willing woman.

Lucien felt naive and so, so stupid for not realising that hours ago. He was such an idiot. Of *course* Dean would prefer her to him. She was probably fun and sociable. They must have so much in common. Why would Dean ever want Lucien when he could have someone like that?

Lucien knew he was spiralling spectacularly when he started picturing her as Rafael's future mother. What if Dean married her? What if Dean wanted to move her in here? What if Dean was falling in love with her right now?

The whisky burned his throat, and he slid the bottle back on its shelf. He didn't want to get drunk. He wanted to watch sad old films on TV and feel sorry for himself.

He browsed through the movies, selected one, then snuggled down into the cushions.

Lucien rarely understood people at the best of times, but he had been sure that Dean was attracted to him. There had been too many moments between them. Moments that had meant something. When the air between them had felt hot and charged and laden with possibility. But, as open a person as Dean was, Lucien had the feeling there was something Dean was holding back. Something Dean hadn't told him, or maybe even something Dean didn't know himself.

Whatever it was, it was stopping Dean from letting Lucien all the way in. And, try as he might, Lucien couldn't fully ignore that tiny voice inside him telling him that Dean might be holding back because Lucien wasn't good enough for him. Or for Rafael.

Lucien finally fell asleep, exhausted, hugging a cushion and unable to deny to himself that he was nursing an enormous crush on his house mate.

Dean and Jenny left together, stepping out into the cool, refreshing air. Dean waited at the pub as Jenny walked the few steps to her house and unlocked the front door. She tripped up the step slightly, then giggled and waved at him, before disappearing inside.

Dean smiled, then checked his phone and cursed under his breath. He'd had no idea it was so late.

Dean sobered up completely on the cold walk home. His breath made clouds in front of his face, and he shoved his hands in his pockets to try to stave off the cold. On the way through the streets, following the quietly babbling brook, he thought about what Lucien had said. About how Dean was the only one who accepted the real him. He couldn't imagine why anyone would want to change a thing about Lucien. He was perfect.

He suddenly couldn't wait to see him. They'd had this one solitary evening. They could have spent it alone together, without any little voices asking to be played with or refusing to go to bed, and he'd spent it with a stranger. There was only one person he wanted to be with, and only one place where he could finally finish that kiss they'd started. He hoped he hadn't missed his chance.

Dean broke out into a jog.

His body tingled with a rush of pleasant heat when he finally stepped inside the front door. He hung up his jacket and as soon as he reached the living room spotted Lucien lying on the sofa. Damn it, he was too late. Lucien was fast asleep.

Dean crossed the room and reached out to shake Lucien's shoulder, but then thought better of it. He looked so peaceful lying there, his face completely relaxed and his thick hair even messier than usual.

Lucien would get a bad back if he spent much longer lying in that position… Dean made a decision. He would shoot upstairs to get changed, then come back down, gently wake Lucien and make them both some hot chocolate before bed. They could at least enjoy a conversation, or sit and watch TV together on the sofa for a little while on this, their one and only night without Dean's mini-me.

As he ran up the stairs he noticed something blue out of the corner of his eye, but ignored it, keen to get out of his cold denim jeans and into something more comfy, so he could go back downstairs with Lucien. He looked so warm and soft on the sofa, and something inside Dean just wanted to snuggle up next to him and nest.

He threw his clothes in the hamper and pulled on his comfiest sweatpants and an old, faded hoodie over his T-shirt. On his way back downstairs, he actually focused on what the blue thing was and stopped dead. Why the hell was there a huge gift bow on Lucien's office door? Was someone else here? Did Lucien have someone over who'd got him a gift and put it in his office? Was it Lucien's birthday?

Dean tilted his head, staring at the incongruous bow. He should probably just go and ask Lucien, but something drew him over to the door. He'd just take a little peek to see what was up…

When he opened the door, he knew immediately what was up. It couldn't be anything else. Lucien had made Rafael a bedroom.

A lamp threw warm, cosy light over the whole room, there was a new bed, new curtains and a matching rug, and the wall was Rafael's favourite shade of blue, for God's sake. How had Lucien even done this? *When* had he done this? It was like a tiny miracle. It must have taken so much time and planning and effort.

Dean felt his heart expand, too big to fit in his chest, and he turned to run down the stairs. But then he stopped.

Lucien had done all this tonight. Alone.

That was why Lucien had fallen asleep on the sofa—partly from exhaustion, and partly because he must have been waiting up excitedly for Dean, so he could show him what he'd done. Lucien had put a bow on the door and everything. And Dean had ruined it all by being late home.

He felt the heart that had just that moment expanded break. He felt terrible. But touched beyond words.

Binxie jumped out of the shadows and rubbed against his ankles, so Dean reached down and grabbed her on his way to Lucien. Maybe things would go better if he brought a beloved gift.

He turned off the TV, tentatively deposited Binxie on Lucien's lap and knelt down by his side. He looked so sweet asleep, gently snoring… Dean whispered Lucien's name and gently touched his bare arm.

Lucien twitched and snuffled into his cushion, before slowly opening his eyes. 'Dean…' He gazed up at Dean for a moment, before blinking and sitting upright. 'You're home.' Lucien's eyes slid away. 'How was your date?'

'It wasn't a date.'

Why did everyone keep calling it that? And why wasn't Lucien maintaining eye contact?

Dean must have really made a misstep by not coming home sooner.

'How was your not-date?' Lucien mumbled.

'It was a nightmare, to be honest. And I'm glad it's over.'

Lucien gave a small smile, and Dean took that as a tentative win.

'I missed you.' Dean couldn't hold it in any longer.

Lucien's smile turned into a confused frown. 'You missed me?'

Dean nodded.

'Why?'

'I always miss you when you're not around,' Dean said quietly. 'Also, if I'd been home, instead of out, I could have helped you do what you've done upstairs.'

Lucien blushed right before Dean's eyes. They were so close that Dean saw the colour bloom over his cheeks and even up to his temples.

'You saw?'

Dean nodded. 'I don't know what to say, Lucien. I'm speechless.'

'Do you think he'll like it?'

'He'll love it.'

'He doesn't have to move in there if he doesn't want to. He probably likes being with you at night.'

'No, no he hates it. I snore.'

Lucien snorted out a laugh. 'Oh, that's unfortunate.'

'No one's ever done anything like this for me

before. I mean for Rafael. You did it for Rafael, not me.'

Smooth, Dean. He tried not to roll his eyes at himself.

'I did it for both of you.' Lucien shrugged one shoulder. 'It's nothing, really.'

'It's everything. Stay right where you are. I'm making us hot chocolate.'

'I can do it.'

An image of the mess Lucien had managed to make with pancakes flashed through Dean's mind. And, as adorable as that would be to see again, he shook his head.

'You just DIYed your little heart out—the least I can do is make you a drink.'

'That's true,' said Lucien, grabbing another cushion and shoving it under his head.

He lay back on the couch and watched as Dean returned to the kitchen. He grabbed a pan, some milk and cream from the fridge, and some chocolate to melt. He was going to give Lucien the best hot chocolate he'd ever had.

'We have powdered stuff in the cupboard,' called Lucien.

Dean slapped his hand over his heart, mock-offended.

'Powdered? Wait till you taste this—it'll change your life.'

Ten minutes later, Dean poured smooth, steaming chocolate into two large mugs. He sprinkled pink and white marshmallows on top, then carried them through to Lucien.

Lucien sat up and accepted his mug with a shy smile, cupping his hands around it, warming them. 'Thank you. This looks so delicious. Would it be rude to down it in one?'

'It would require a visit to A&E. Blow on it for a while first. It's too hot—you'll burn your tongue.'

Dean made a face at himself. Way to sound like a dad.

Lucien obediently blew on his hot chocolate, and Dean put his mug on the coffee table so he could reach over and grab a blanket from the far end of the sofa. Deciding not to overthink it, he threw the blanket over both their laps and moved closer to Lucien. He put the TV on to create some background noise, but rather than face the screen he shifted to face Lucien, and watched as he tentatively sipped his drink.

'I can't believe you kept it all a secret,' said Dean. 'I didn't know you had it in you.'

'I'm quite sneaky.'

Dean laughed. 'Who knew?'

But then he was reminded of the secret he was keeping, and it didn't seem so funny any more. He wished so hard that he could tell Lucien the truth. If he knew then Dean could enjoy this closeness without being scared that it would be ripped away at any moment.

His heart raced as he realised it might be time to tell him everything. How could Dean be any more sure that Lucien was safe to be around Rafael? What was he still waiting for?

He took a long swallow of hot chocolate.

'The bed was hidden in the shed for days,' said Lucien. 'I was nervous one of you would find it.'

'I didn't even know we had a shed.'

'Then I guess I'm lucky you're so oblivious.'

Dean opened his mouth, not sure what he was going to say, but intending somehow to tell Lucien the truth. But before he could speak Lucien interrupted him.

'This is so nice. I haven't felt this relaxed in months.'

'You haven't?' Dean responded weakly.

'Normally I only fully relax when I'm alone. Being around people, however much I like them, usually makes me feel on edge. But you're different, somehow.' Lucien turned towards Dean, mirroring his position, and settled his head against the back of the sofa. 'You make me feel really calm.'

'Just call me Diazepam,' Dean joked.

Lucien smiled lazily, his eyes hooded, and continued to gaze up at Dean. 'I'm cold.'

Dean pulled the blanket further over Lucien, up to his waist, and tucked it around him. Then he took a breath and bravely snuggled closer, pressing their thighs together under the blanket. Dean's hand remained trapped underneath the warm fabric and he flexed it, itching to reach over and make contact with Lucien.

Lucien finished his drink, then eyed Dean's empty mug. He removed it gently from Dean's grip and placed them both on the coffee table. As he leaned forward Dean caught a faint trace of his shampoo, and sensed the solid weight of his body as he passed him. When Lucien settled back into position, he seemed even closer.

Dean swallowed, ultra-aware of Lucien's warmth, of their bodies, touching now all the way from shoulder to knee in a burning hot line of firm contact.

Dean pushed down his intention to tell Lucien everything. It could wait a few hours at least. He should give Lucien one last stress-free evening before he ruined it.

'Are you sure about losing your office?' Dean asked. 'It's one of your last private spaces—the only place you can hide from me.'

Lucien glanced up, and something in Dean's chest went a little askew when he looked into Lucien's eyes from so close a distance. Black eyelashes framed grey eyes the colour of storm clouds…clouds currently crackling with electricity. Heat emanated from Lucien's body and Dean couldn't help but lean in.

Lucien drew a breath as Dean got closer, and his eyes flicked down to Dean's lips. Did that mean what Dean thought it did? Dean licked his own lips quickly, and Lucien's pupils dilated.

'I don't want to hide from you any more,' Lucien whispered.

Dean had a moment of doubt. What was he thinking? He shouldn't be doing this. It was too risky. But Lucien was so close, and so warm and so soft. And so beautiful. It would be the easiest thing in the world for Dean to move a little closer and finally feel Lucien's lips on his.

So he did.

Lucien seemed frozen in shock—but only for a moment. He soon kissed back, soothing Dean's nerves and eagerly kissing away his worry that he'd misinterpreted everything.

Lucien cradled Dean's face in his hands, his thumb stroking over the soft skin of his cheek until it made Dean shiver. It was crystal-clear that Lucien wasn't anywhere near the man Dean had thought he was when they met. Lucien would stop at nothing to help not only his patients, but also the people he cared about. His walls had just been protecting the vulnerable man underneath.

Lucien stroked his fingers lightly all the way up Dean's arm, giving him goosebumps, and then he gripped Dean's neck as they kissed. Dean moaned into Lucien's mouth. Lucien grasped Dean around the waist and heaved him closer. Dean found himself sprawled on Lucien's lap, his knees straddling Lucien's thighs.

'Hi,' Dean whispered, smiling against Lucien's lips.

Lucien gripped Dean's waist tighter. 'Should we take this upstairs?'

Those words sent a thrill up Dean's spine, and he nodded breathlessly. 'Yes, please.'

CHAPTER SEVEN

EVER SINCE DEAN had kissed him, everything had happened on pure instinct—almost without thought. When his brain finally kicked in Lucien tried to get as close to Dean as he could, and found himself with the exquisite weight of Dean's body in his lap.

He gazed into Dean's eyes and reached forward to kiss his beautiful soft mouth—because apparently he was allowed to do that now. Dean kissed him back—hard—and Lucien explored Dean's body, running his hands up Dean's thighs and over his solid, muscular chest, enjoying the broad expanse of his back and squeezing his thick upper arms. All the while Dean gripped Lucien's hair and kissed slowly up his neck towards his ear. Heat and pleasure flared through Lucien's body.

Upstairs. Yes. They needed to be there as soon as possible.

He shifted Dean into place, wrapped his arms firmly around his waist and stood up. Dean gasped and held on tighter, wrapping his long legs around Lucien's back.

'Oh, wow…' Dean whispered, almost too quietly for Lucien to hear.

They somehow made it up one flight of stairs, stumbling most of the way, unable to keep their hands off each other long enough to concentrate on walking. Lucien wondered for a moment whose room they should head to, but then Dean pulled him through a door, kicked it shut and slammed Lucien up against it, pressing him into the wood and kissing him with a surprising sweetness for someone so fired up.

It looked as if they were choosing Lucien's room.

Lucien got his hands caught up in Dean's shirt and tried to say something, but Dean's kisses made it indecipherable.

Dean pulled away. 'What?'

'I said, you're wearing too many clothes.'

Dean grinned and yanked his shirt off over his head, dropping it to the floor. Then he helped Lucien out of his.

Lucien couldn't wait any longer, and pushed Dean back on to his bed, immediately crawling after him and covering him with his body. When his knee slipped between Dean's thighs, pushing them apart, he could feel that Dean was just as excited as he was.

It struck him that he was living out in Technicolor all the things he had been scared Dean would be doing with someone else that night. He felt thoroughly embarrassed over his earlier spiral into despair, but was pleasantly rescued from his thoughts when Dean sucked his lower lip into his mouth and bit it softly. It sent sparks shooting through his body and a hot jolt of lust.

'You taste so good,' Dean whispered.

Lucien wondered fleetingly if it was possible to die from pleasure, and he felt his cheeks blush pink.

'Look at you…' Dean breathed reverently.

All Lucien could do was look back.

Then Dean licked into his mouth and proceeded to take him apart.

Later, feeling sated, sweaty and completely boneless, Lucien wrapped his arms around Dean and tugged his warmth tight to him.

He held him close like a limpet and decided simply never to let go…

Dean woke up first, blinking in the early-morning sunlight. Only to find a sleeping Lucien facing him. Their fingers were entwined between them on the pillow.

He'd never held someone's hand in his sleep before.

He listened to Lucien's even breaths and smiled to himself when he felt the soft twitch of Lucien's fingers as he dreamed. Pretty adorable for a guy who could lift Dean up and carry him around as if he weighed nothing at all.

Christ, that had been hot.

Dean was so warm and comfy he drifted back to sleep, and when he awoke again he found it was Lucien's turn to stare at him. He reached out to cover Lucien's eyes, and Lucien pulled away, laughing.

'Let me look.'

'Why should I?'

'I was counting your freckles.'

'Oh.' Dean shyly hid his face in the pillow. 'I have too many.'

'I love them.' Lucien cleared his throat. 'Do you…regret anything about last night?'

'Yes…'

'Oh.'

Lucien's face fell. Dean could tell from the line that appeared between his eyebrows that he was worried, so he finished his sentence quickly. 'I regret you sitting alone all night when I could have been here with you.'

'Oh.' This time Lucien smiled.

'By the way, I think Helen knows about us.'

'What? How? It's only just happened. Even *she's* not that good.'

'She saw it before we did, I guess. We talked about you the other day at work. I also heard some very interesting stories about your early days as a GP,' Dean teased.

'Oh, God.' Lucien ducked under the covers for a moment. 'Maybe I don't hide my feelings as well as I thought I did.'

'I'm starting to think you're not the only one,' said Dean.

'I don't like people very often, you know.'

Dean nodded. 'I know. I don't know why the hell you like me. But I'm glad you do.'

Even if it probably wouldn't last long once he knew the truth.

'I can't imagine how anyone *couldn't* like you. How anyone could work with you every day, or pass you once in the street, and not fall irreversibly in lust with you for the rest of their lives.'

Dean's face grew hot and he squirmed away. 'Shut up.'

Lucien grabbed him around the waist and yanked him effortlessly back against him. Dean's back slammed against Lucien's chest and he lost his breath for a moment.

'Careful,' murmured Dean. 'Or we might need to have round two.'

'Don't threaten me with a good time,' Lucien whispered hotly into the back of Dean's neck.

Ten minutes after the best round two of Dean's life, Dean waited for Lucien to finish using the shower so he could have a turn. He could have climbed the stairs and used his own shower, but he didn't want to be a whole floor away from Lucien. How pathetic was that?

Dean sighed and ran a hand over his face. This had got very serious, very fast.

In the kitchen, Lucien kissed Dean's forehead as he passed him his coffee. Not for the first time, Dean's heart did a little flip at how adorable Lucien looked first thing in the morning, rubbing his sleepy eyes with one hand, then trying to tame hair that was even wilder than usual with the other.

As Dean cooked breakfast Lucien hugged him from behind and nuzzled his neck, while Dean talked him softly through how not to burn eggs and bacon.

Dean felt safe and special and cared for. But he couldn't enjoy the moment as much as he longed to.

Dean couldn't avoid it any longer. He knew it was finally time to tell Lucien. But that realisation didn't stop his chest tightening with nerves when he considered what Lucien's reaction might be to the truth.

Now that he had developed feelings for Lucien he was terrified that he would reject Dean for keeping the secret for so long. And, worse, he might reject Rafael along with him—all because of Dean's actions. And why shouldn't he? Dean wasn't good enough for Lucien. After all, everyone in his life had left him—why would Lucien be any different? Sooner or later he'd realise that he deserved someone better than Dean.

But, regardless of that, it was time. Dean resolved to tell him the truth and take whatever consequences came his way. He would do it after Rafael's birthday party. He couldn't risk ruining his son's big day.

CHAPTER EIGHT

SINCE LUCIEN AND Dean had spent the night together things had been a little strange. They'd had that one wonderful night, and an even better morning-after, but since then nothing. Dean was still affectionate, and funny, and sweet—just like always. But there was something between them. As if Dean was holding something back.

Lucien tried not to worry about it, even though some traitorous part of him worried that Dean regretted sleeping with Lucien.

Maybe he was sick of country life and bored with being stuck with Lucien all the time. Maybe he wanted more space for Rafael. Or a family home without a random stranger in it.

Although Lucien hoped he wasn't a random stranger any more. To either of them.

Lucien smiled as he remembered Rafael's reaction to his new room.

'Daddy says some people don't like hugs so you have to ask first,' he'd said.

Lucien had smiled. 'That's exactly right.'

'Would you like a hug, please?'

Lucien had blinked down at Rafael and realised he would—very much. And when they'd hugged Lucien had felt something deep inside him click into place.

'It's the best room I've ever seen!' Rafael had told him. 'Blue is my favourite colour!'

'I heard it might be.'

'I'm heading into work. I'll see you later.'

Lucien just managed to put down his toast before he had an armful of Dean. Dean hugged him tightly around the middle and Lucien squeezed Dean's shoulders close to him, breathing in his scent.

Dean spoke into Lucien's neck. 'I'll start setting up for the party when I get home. Hopefully I'll have most of it done by the time you finish work.'

'You don't have to. I can help with it when I get back. Not that I know the first thing about children's parties.'

Dean leaned back to peck him on the lips, then stepped away. Lucien immediately missed his warmth.

Dean smiled. 'I'll teach you.'

With that, he grabbed his bag and left.

Almost at the end of a long shift, during which Dean spent all his breaks planning last-minute touches for Rafael's party, Dean's last patient of the day shuffled into his consulting room and sat down, clutching a backpack on her lap. Dean skimmed through her notes on his monitor. An eighteen-year-old named Lydia.

'What can I do for you today?' Dean asked, smiling warmly and trying in vain to make eye contact.

'I normally see Dr Benedict,' Lydia mumbled at the floor.

'I hear that a lot.' Dean smiled. 'But I'm afraid he's not in right now, so can I try to help?'

She sighed deeply, and Dean waited for her to speak.

'I've not been feeling very well lately.'

'Okay. Can you tell me more about that?'

'I didn't want to come here today,' said Lydia.

Dean waited patiently for her to continue.

'I just wanted to stay at home. It's safe there. But my dad was the same as me. He died because he didn't get treated, and I don't want to be like him.'

'That's very brave, Lydia. I'm sorry about your dad.' Dean glanced again at Lydia's records on his screen. 'When did he pass away?'

'Last year.'

'Sadly, it's still very common for men not to feel comfortable asking for help with their mental health.'

Lydia nodded and stared down at her hands.

'Anyway, you've done the right thing coming in. We're always here for you.'

'I don't want to bother you with something stupid.'

'If you've got symptoms you're concerned about, you shouldn't be struggling with that alone. That's exactly what we're here for.'

She shifted in her seat. 'I've been hearing things.'

'What kind of things?'

'Whispers. Constant whispering. Telling me things.'

Dean nodded. 'What kind of things are they telling you?'

'That you're a terrible doctor, and this is completely useless, and you won't be able to help me.' She finally made eye contact. 'And I bet they're right.'

Dean tilted his head.

'And I have a knife.'

Dean glanced at her hands. She wasn't holding anything.

He kept his voice calm. 'What are you saying, Lydia?'

'I'm not saying anything. I just have a knife.'

'Where is it?'

'In my bag.'

'What are you planning on doing with it?'

'Nothing. But I could if I had to.'

A patient had once brought a gun into Dean's

last practice, so he had learned to take any mention of a weapon very seriously. They'd even had a panic button installed after that, which had triggered the police to attend immediately. Not that there was anything like that here.

'Is something happening at home, Lydia? Is that why you feel you need a knife? For protection?'

She shook her head.

Dean turned his chair to face her dead-on, keeping some distance between them but wanting her to know he was fully engaged. 'Do you feel that I am a threat to you? Would you prefer to speak with a different doctor?'

She shook her head again. 'I'm not going to hurt you, or myself, if that's what you're thinking. The whispers say someone's trying to kill me. But they don't think it's you.'

The 'whispers' rang a bell. A very specific bell.

'I'm just going to check something on my screen for a second. Is that okay?'

She nodded, and Dean pulled his chair closer to his desk. He went back through Lydia's notes and found what he was looking for after a minute. She had suffered from paranoid hallucinations two years previously, but they'd receded when she'd been prescribed anti-psychotic meds. He would bet good money she was the patient Lucien had been worried about in the staff room on his first day at the surgery. And apparently the hallucinations were back.

'Have you been taking your Olanzapine as normal, Lydia?'

She avoided his gaze.

'Have you stopped taking it?'

Her lack of an answer likely meant yes.

'Have you been attending your CBT sessions?'

'I'm still on the waiting list for those.'

Damn. Those waiting lists could be months or even years long.

'Have you been having problems sleeping lately? Or eating?'

She squeezed her bag tighter. 'This is the first time I've left the house in weeks.'

Dean's heart sank. He felt terrible for her. She looked pale and drawn and absolutely exhausted.

'You've been really brave coming here today,' he told her. 'It must have felt like a huge step, and you did exactly the right thing. I don't think you're coping very well, and I think you need some help.' Dean stood. 'I'm really proud of you for coming in. Listen, you stay here. I'm going to get you a drink of water, and then we'll see what we can do to help you.'

Dean found Helen out in the corridor. 'Can you keep an eye on my patient for a second? I'm going to use the HCP line and call an ambulance for her. She's suffering from auditory hallucinations, she's paranoid and she semi-threatened me with a theoretical knife.'

'How is a knife theoretical?'

'She said she has one in her bag, but I'm not convinced.'

'Well, that's a dangerous assumption.'

Dean strongly suspected his hunch was right, but it was better to be safe than sorry.

'Okay. Stay outside the room, but watch the door. I'll ask her if I can check her bag when I get back.'

Dean made his phone call from the reception desk and poured Lydia a drink from the water cooler. His mobile phone vibrated in his pocket and he automatically checked it. It was Rafael's school. It must be an emergency, or they wouldn't call him at work.

He answered immediately, his heart in his mouth. But his panic soon faded when they simply asked him to verify his home address. Apparently they had the postcode wrong. He corrected it, then rolled his eyes as he quickly ended the call and rushed back to his room.

Only to find it empty, and no Helen either.

'Er...where is my patient?' he called out.

'Would that be the one who's absconded to the car park?' Helen shouted from the end of the corridor.

'What?'

Dean dropped the cup of water and ran. He

found Helen standing in the back doorway, waiting for him, and they ran outside together to the grassy lawn by the car park. Dean shaded his eyes from the sun with one hand and squinted at Lydia, standing under a weeping willow.

'Fancied some fresh air?'

Dean crossed the lawn towards her and nearly tripped over her backpack, his foot catching in the strap. She laughed at him, seemingly shocking even herself, and Dean smiled back.

'Since it's nearly killed me, may I have your permission to have a look through your bag?'

'Go for it,' she said, then sat down cross-legged on the grass.

Dean carefully looked through the almost empty bag. There was no knife that he could see.

'So, why are we out here?'

'Did you call the police on me?'

'No, I didn't. I've called for a ride to take us to the hospital. They have specialists there who can help you.'

'Us?'

'Yes, I'm coming with you.'

Some of the tension seemed to leave the frame of her shoulders. She pulled up some grass from the lawn and tossed it away from them.

'Who says I want you to come?'

'No one. But I want to make sure you get there safe.'

She threw a few more handfuls of grass, then seemed to run out of steam.

'Was there a reason you left the consulting room?' Dean asked.

'The whispers were too loud in there. I needed to be outside.' She turned her face up to the sun. 'The wind in the trees sometimes drowns them out.'

Dean sat back against the tree and listened to the rustling willow. The dancing tips of its branches almost touched the lawn in a green curtain, shielding them from the world.

'I'll sit here with you for a while. But we'll need to get up when the ambulance arrives.'

Lydia didn't answer, and when Dean looked over she was swaying back and forth slightly, with her eyes shut and her hands over her ears.

She must be experiencing the auditory hallucinations again.

Dean felt terrible. If he hadn't answered that call from the school he would probably have been back with Lydia, and she never would have ended up panicking and running out.

He waited patiently until Lydia took down her hands and opened her eyes. 'You okay?' he asked.

She gulped and looked away. 'I've been better.'

At that moment the ambulance pulled around the corner into the car park.

* * *

When Lucien arrived at the surgery, Helen accosted him.

'Did Dean contact you?'

'No. Why?'

'I'll let him tell you all about it later. Long story short: he's at the hospital with a patient, but he should be done soon.'

'I hope so—it's Rafael's party today.'

'Oh, it'll be fine. That's hours away,' said Helen.

But on his break Lucien found himself distracted by wondering whether Dean was home yet or not, so he decided to stop wondering and just text him.

How are you doing? Helen's wondering where you are. I couldn't care less, obviously...

Dean immediately replied.

I was just about to message you. Lol, btw. We're waiting to be seen. There's a big backlog.

Lucien sighed. It wasn't hugely surprising news, but it was unfortunate on the one day Dean needed to get back.

Sorry to hear that. Who is the patient?

It's the patient we discussed the other day. The one you were worried about.

Lucien's body tensed, and he sat up straight in his chair.

Is she okay?

I'll explain more later, but she's safe. She says hello. Or she would if she wasn't currently ignoring me and playing on her phone.

Damn it. Lucien should have done more for her when he'd had the opportunity. He hadn't stopped thinking of her since her aunt had spoken to him in the shop. But he was always trying so hard to avoid crossing that line.

She's my patient. I should come in and swap places with you, then you can come back and get on with the party.

No... I appreciate the offer, but I'm here now. Despite what I just said, we are actually getting on. But things are a bit delicate. I want to stay.

Lucien loved it that Dean was so dedicated. But it couldn't help but remind him of his mother, the uncrowned queen of crossing that line. He'd loved his mother for how much she cared, how big her heart was, but sometimes, as a child, his not being the main focus of that heart had hurt. And now Dean was doing exactly what Lucien's mother would have done. Missing his son's birthday party by putting the patient first.

Dean went on.

I'll have plenty of time to do everything. Don't worry.

When Lucien didn't reply, Dean typed:

You still there?

I'm here. Listen, Lydia can be tricky to deal with. But I'll tell you one thing I learned about her. She hates being treated with kid gloves. So don't talk down to her, and don't ever lie to her. Talk to her like an adult and be brutally honest.

Okay. Thanks, Lucien.

Message me if you need anything at all.

I will!

Lucien had a bad feeling that Dean was being way too optimistic about making it back in time to do everything he'd planned for the party…

* * *

Dean brought two horribly weak teas from the cafeteria, and carefully handed one to Lydia. 'Have you been able to talk to anyone about the way you're feeling? Family? Friends?'

'My mum always tells me to stop being so self-absorbed. And that she knew from day one I'd be more trouble than I was worth.'

Dean fought a flare of anger. He always tried to be kind in the face of cruelty. Her mother might well have her own issues. But to say that to your own child…

Lydia really didn't have anyone to advocate for her.

Dean settled down next to Lydia and tried to stop obsessing over Rafael's party. Up until six months ago, all Dean had had to focus on was his job. The old Dean hadn't thought anything on Earth could be more fulfilling than advocating for his patients. But now he'd found something else that made him feel just as worthwhile, if not more.

Had he been a better doctor pre-Rafael? Was he now giving his patients less than they deserved as well as his son? He still wanted to be the best doctor he could be, but not if that meant short-changing Rafael. Surely it was possible to do both.

A little later Dean looked at his watch. Lydia had gone to use the bathroom ten minutes ago.

Something didn't feel right.

Dean walked around the corner and knocked on the bathroom door.

'Lydia?'

No answer.

Dean wasn't above braving entry into the women's bathroom if the situation called for it, but a gentler approach was probably best here.

This time he tapped gently on the door. 'Lydia, I just need to know if you're in there. You don't have to talk to me or come out.'

'I'm in here.'

'Cool.' Dean felt a wave of relief. 'Are you okay?'

'The fan in here drowns them out.'

Dean nodded in understanding. She was hearing the whispers again.

'I just want to go home.' Lydia sounded exhausted.

'I know. I'm sorry this is taking so long.' Dean made a decision. 'If you're happy in there for a minute, I'm going to see if I can hurry things along a bit.'

Lydia answered by turning on the hand-dryer.

Finally Dean located the right person to talk to, and cornered him at the desk. The man looked at his screen for a moment before responding to Dean.

'There are a number of patients that need to be seen first. She may not be seen today.'

'It's fine, Dr Vasquez.'

Lydia appeared from behind Dean.

'It's okay. I'll just go home. I can come back another day. Maybe Mum will come with me.'

'Absolutely not. Leave this to me.'

Dean sent Lydia back to her seat, out of earshot, and then turned back to the man, making sure he spoke calmly and clearly.

'She needs to be seen today. My patient is suffering from auditory hallucinations and has a history of psychosis. She needs help now.'

He stared at Dean for a long moment and heaved a huge, soul-deep sigh.

'There might be something I can do. Hold on.'

An hour later, Lucien received a message from Dean.

They're assessing her now. Psychiatric evaluation.

Is she coping okay? At least she's being seen. Does this mean you're free to leave?

Not yet. I told her I'd be here when she finished. I can't leave her alone. She doesn't have anyone else here. I'm responsible for her. I feel so guilty. I was on the phone and she slipped out of the clinic.

Yes, Helen filled me in about that. But it wasn't

your fault. You sit tight and let me know if anything changes.

Lucien checked his watch. Time was really ticking down now. Dean was never going to make it back in time to set up the party.

Lucien didn't want to stress Dean out further, so in a break between patients he pulled up Google on his monitor and searched 'party for seven-year-old'. He read for a minute, his eyes growing bigger by the second.

Yeah, he was never going to be able to do any of that by himself.

'Helen! I need serious help,' he called.

Helen rushed in, holding a steaming bowl of instant noodles and a spoon.

'Sorry, I didn't know you were eating.'

'Spit it out, Lucien.'

'Dean's still stuck at the hospital. We might have to throw Rafael's party for him.'

Helen's eyes widened. 'Oh, fudge...' She thought for about three seconds. 'Okay. Look, I'm going to call an emergency locum. I'll switch all your remaining appointments to them. Then we can both handle this situation together. You may have years of experience in medicine, but you don't know real trauma until you've been surrounded by fifteen screaming kids, high on juice and chocolate cake.'

She swung Lucien's monitor to face her, rolled

her eyes at the Google search and clicked over to his schedule.

'You'll have to see the next two patients—it's too late for changes. I'll get hold of the locum.' She rushed out, calling back over her shoulder, 'You can't learn anything you need to know about kids' parties online. You need an expert in the field. And that's me!'

Thank God for Helen.

Just as Lucien finished up with his last patient of the day, his phone dinged with a message.

They're referring her to the local crisis team, but they won't be here for a couple of hours. I'm going to stay and wait with her.

Lucien sighed.

With any luck they'll turn up sooner than that and I can rush home.

Lucien answered.

Don't worry about Rafael's party I can handle it.

What? How?

You tell me what you had planned and I'll do it. With a little help from Helen.

Lucien, you can't do that.

Of course we can. It won't be as good as you doing it, but it'll be better than nothing.

This is my first time doing a kid's party too, don't forget. I was probably going to make a mess of it anyway.

Lucien had forgotten.

This was Rafael's first birthday with Dean, and the first without his mother.

Lucien's heart hurt. And with that came an absolute determination that he was going to make this party the best he possibly could.

He got a new message.

Are we making a mistake? Should we cancel the party?

No!

We could postpone for week. I can call round all the parents.

But we're already having it the day before his actual birthday so that his best friend can come. It has to be today. He's all excited about it now. He'll be crushed if we cancel.

Rafael had been practically vibrating with excitement all week about his big party. This morning Lucien had been sure he would either explode or pass out.

He typed out a new message.

I promise it'll be fine.

Maybe. I guess with enough cake and sweets Rafael will be off his head anyway.

That's more or less what Helen said.

Okay. Look, I'm still planning on getting back for the party. So you get things started and I can help when I get there.

Sounds like a plan.

Dean proceeded to send him instructions for decorations, food, games and party bags. He also rang Rafael's school and told them that Lucien would be collecting him.

It had not escaped Lucien's notice that Dean was continuing this whole conversation by text. Most people would have switched to a phone call by now, but Dean knew Lucien didn't love talking on the phone and had noticed he avoided it wherever possible, so he hadn't even suggested it.

It gave Lucien a warm, looked-after feeling in

his chest. And along with that, a burst of confidence.

He could handle this.

Three hours later, Lucien saw how wrong he had been.

Most of the children were playing on a deafeningly loud karaoke machine with two microphones. Lucien's face hurt from all the encouraging smiles he had to fake every time a child finished what could only loosely be called a song. Rafael and the remainder of his guests were sprawled on the floor playing a video game, only three feet away from the karaoke machine, all whilst talking, screaming, and laughing hysterically.

How any of them could hear anything was some kind of miracle. Because Lucien couldn't even hear himself think.

Lucien had been lulled into a false sense of security when the party had started off quietly. Polite, well-dressed children had handed Rafael presents wrapped by their parents. They'd even played some games, led by Helen, like musical statues and pass the parcel—the parcel made in about five minutes by Helen herself, whom Lucien was beginning to suspect was some sort of magical fairy godmother sent from heaven.

He'd been stunned that kids still played the sort of games he remembered from his own childhood. And he'd texted Dean to tell him so. He also sent a couple of pictures of Rafael enjoying himself, knowing Dean must feel awful, stuck at the hospital, missing all this.

Dean had replied with a question.

How did the food go down?

Dean had pre-ordered a birthday cake and a mountain of tiny sandwiches on platters, and they'd been delivered about an hour before the party started. Helen had brought a couple of shopping bags full of sweets and crisps with her from the supermarket, dumped them on the table and told Lucien to fill up all the bowls he had and make them look pretty.

Lucien had shown Helen the decorations Dean had bought. Blue and purple balloons, a blue one-use tablecloth with superheroes on, purple paper cups and plates and a huge *Happy Birthday* banner. By the time Lucien had filled some bowls with sweets and crisps Helen had already put up all the decorations and the house had looked wonderful. Everything had gone perfectly to Dean's plan.

But now the food had been demolished, most of the balloons had been popped, and the entire celebration had descended into chaos.

Lucas answered Dean.

The food went down wonderfully. Everything's perfect.

'Is this normal?' he asked Helen, who was wiping up a spilled drink from the food table.

'Totally and completely,' she said with a blissful smile.

'Are you *enjoying* this?' Lucien asked, trying to keep the incredulity out of his voice and failing.

Helen shrugged. 'I've missed the chaos. My kids just want to go off and see a band with their friends on their birthdays now. I'm lucky if they let me take them out to the shops for a new outfit.'

Rafael chose that moment to grab Lucien's knee with a chocolatey hand and pull himself up on to his lap. He fell heavily against Lucien's chest, and somehow managed to get more chocolate on Lucien's shirt.

'Is Daddy still at the hospital?' he asked sadly.

'Yes.' Lucien decided Rafael deserved to smother his shirt in as much chocolate as he pleased. 'Did you want to talk to him again?'

Rafael nodded into his chest, so Lucien dialled Dean's number and listened to it ring, then passed the phone to Rafael, wincing only slightly as it got covered in chocolate fingerprints.

Helen eyed the stains and patted his shoulder. 'Enjoy the mess while you can.'

Lucien tried to keep Rafael more or less upright as he shuffled around on his lap. He seemed to find his second wind as he talked to his dad, giggling and throwing himself back and forth with laughter at something Dean said on the phone.

Lucien smiled to himself. Dean did have that sort of effect on people.

After a few minutes Rafael hung up, thrust the phone back at Lucien and shouted a thank-you as he slid off his lap and launched himself back into the video game with his friends.

Another text from Dean came through immediately.

You'll have to put him to bed later. Do you know how?

Lucien thought about it.

I've witnessed a few bedtimes. I can figure it out.

But Lucien suddenly felt nervous. What if Rafael refused to brush his teeth or go to bed without his dad there? What if he didn't like the way Lucien read him his story?

Lucien shook his head. If he could live through the auction, he could manage to put a kid to bed.

Lucien checked the list of activities Dean had sent him. It was piñata time.

Lucien left the kids with Helen, then got a ladder and hung the piñata from a thick, high branch in the garden. He'd probably have been given this job even if Dean were here, he thought, seeing as Dean hated heights so much.

His hands were freezing by the time he managed to tie a decent knot, and he wished he'd worn gloves.

The kids gleefully bashed the living daylights out of the poor rainbow-coloured unicorn. And when all the sweets had disappeared into hungry, grasping hands Rafael and his best friend ran towards the tree trunk at full speed, as if to start climbing it.

Lucien grabbed Rafael around the waist and pulled him gently away, directing him and his friend back towards the kitchen and the table of treats.

'I'll get the ladder and take it down later. No climbing trees today, please.'

Rafael grumbled, but didn't argue, and Lucien silently congratulated himself on not having caused any tantrums so far today.

There was still plenty of time, though.

'How're you doing?' asked Helen, back in the kitchen.

'Remarkably well… I think?'

Helen nodded in agreement. 'It's a miracle—judging from your previous record with kids.'

Lucien had to agree. Only a couple of weeks ago he would hardly have recognised himself.

Now there was only one job left to do. The whole reason Dean had arranged for the party to be in the evening was so it would be dark enough for fireworks to end the night. He'd even pushed notes through all the neighbours' doors and made an announcement on the village Facebook group that there would be fireworks that night, so people should get their cats and dogs in.

Lucien set off the fireworks without a hitch—mainly because he was ably assisted by Helen. Nobody got a sparkler injury, no fireworks smashed through anyone's windows, no cars or trees were set alight by a stray spark.

All things considered, the whole night had gone wonderfully.

Only one kid had thrown up, and that had been in the kitchen, so it was an easy wipe-up. Binxie had been happily set up in Lucien's bedroom for the night, and had never minded fireworks anyway.

After the fireworks Lucien sat on the sofa in the living room, exhausted, holding a huge bowl of popcorn on his lap and surrounded by kids coming down from a sugar high. He looked around. Half of them were asleep, and half were still watching a Disney movie on TV, occasionally scooping a tiny handful of popcorn from the bowl, their eyes never leaving the screen.

People did this every single *year*? Several times over if they had more than one child?

Inconceivable.

Helen tiptoed into the room. 'The parents should

start arriving for pick-up soon. Help me finish the party bags.'

Lucien nodded wordlessly. He was all talked out.

Thank goodness Dean had arranged the party as a drop-off—he couldn't think of anything worse than having to make conversation with a dozen sets of parents for an entire evening.

'You still holding up okay?' Helen asked, reaching out for Lucien's hand and pulling him from the sea of children snuggled up by his side.

'I think so.'

'You've gone from being a stranger to being these kids' favourite person in one evening.'

'Not a total stranger. I'm the GP for most of them.'

He'd recognised all the kids at the party. He'd seen most of them for colds, fevers or banged knees over the years. He'd even helped the mother of one guest give birth to his younger sibling when she'd gone into premature labour during a home visit to her farm just outside the town.

'I found out something today about that one.' He pointed at a sleeping kid on the end of the sofa. 'His younger brother is named after me. I had no idea.'

A year ago Lucien having to talk to all these kids would have been impossible. He would have hidden out in his office rather than face that. Of course he didn't have an office now… But he wasn't missing it. He'd been strangely at ease there, in the middle of a puppy pile of thankfully almost comatose kids.

Once all the children had been picked up, and Helen had gone home clutching the single left-over party bag, Lucien was approached by Rafael, chocolate cake on his face and juice stains on his shirt.

'One more call to Daddy before bed?' asked Lucien.

Rafael nodded and climbed on to the sofa next to him.

Lucien dialled Dean's number and listened to it ring, waiting to pass the phone over to Rafael. But this time there was no answer.

He hung up and texted Dean instead.

Any updates?

After a couple of minutes there was still no answer, and no dots suggesting Dean was typing his reply, so Lucien gave up and tossed his phone on to the sofa.

'Looks like he's either busy getting back, or his phone's out of power.'

Rafael pouted and leaned into Lucien's chest. He found his arms going around the kid naturally, to give him a comforting squeeze.

'He'll be home soon.'

Rafael nodded into Lucien's chest.

'He really missed a great party, didn't he? Lucky we took all those videos and photos to show him what happened.'

Lucien looked around the room at the huge mess that still remained. The gigantic cake still sat on the table. Even with all the kids having seconds, they'd hardly made a dent in it.

'And we saved half of the cake, so we can have a special party with him once he gets back. Or even tomorrow.'

'Not tomorrow! Tonight!'

'Well, we don't know for sure if he'll be back in time.'

Rafael sniffled, and Lucien could sense a meltdown coming.

'Remember it's not your real birthday until tomorrow, so if we do wait until then, that's the day that really counts anyway.'

'It is?'

'Yeah!'

'Do I get more presents?'

'Yes—the ones we saved. From your dad.'

Lucien had let Rafael open the presents from his friends, but had thought Dean would want to be there when he opened the ones from him.

'Oh, yeah!' Rafael had evidently forgotten about those, and he eyed them up now.

'See? Tomorrow will be even better than today.'

On his way to bed, Rafael stopped and stared out of the window.

Lucien nearly tripped over him.

'Can we look in the unicorn to see if we missed some sweets?'

The piñata still swung gently from the branch on the oak tree outside.

'We'll do it tomorrow. It's too cold now.'

Lucien managed to get Rafael tucked up in bed, teeth brushed and pyjamas on, in just under forty-five minutes. He was almost too tired to see the words in the storybook Rafael picked out, and made half of it up, which seemed to both anger and delight Rafael in equal measure.

He was almost convinced Rafael had fallen asleep when he suddenly asked a question. 'Do you love my daddy?'

Lucien was lost for words. He was sure they hadn't kissed in front of Rafael yet, but maybe the kid was smart enough to have recognised that something had changed, or he had noticed on some level that they'd become more comfortable and familiar around each other.

Or maybe they were both just utterly useless at being subtle. So inept that even a six-year-old could see through them.

'Henry has two dads. They go fishing. Can we go fishing?'

Lucien knew he actually needed to answer a question at some point.

'I'm sure we could figure that out,' he managed.

It couldn't be that hard to rent some fishing

rods and find a lake, could it? He had no clue how to fish, but that was what online video tutorials were for.

Back downstairs, Lucien relaxed on the sofa with a cup of tea. The party should have been everything Lucien had been dreading about living in the same house as a child. But he was shocked by how much he'd enjoyed the day, and how close he felt to Rafael.

Dean and Rafael. He couldn't imagine his life without either one of them. He wanted nothing more than to be part of their lives for ever. He didn't know if Dean felt the same way, but he knew he couldn't lose what they had. Lucien needed them both in his life and he would do anything to keep them close.

After what felt like an entire lifetime spent sitting in various waiting rooms and corridors, Dean had got so bored he'd read an entire issue of *Men's Fitness* magazine from 2003 from cover to cover, and posted three stories on Instagram. He'd even started replying to comments, which he normally avoided doing—until he'd realised that was a waste of his battery. He needed to save it to get Lucien and Rafael's updates from the party. They were the only thing keeping him going at the moment.

The last thing he'd heard was that Rafael was

about to go to bed. Dean had officially missed his son's entire birthday party.

He took a breath and tried not to feel like a gigantic failure.

To try and lighten his mood, he subtly pulled his phone out and read through the last few messages from Lucien, laughing under his breath, trying not to let Lydia hear. He didn't want her to know what he was missing to stay with her.

But he wasn't quite subtle enough.

'What is going on? You've been sneaking round corners to talk on your phone and writing messages all night—all the while trying to do it without me noticing. Who are you talking to?'

Dean shoved his phone in his pocket. 'It's nothing important.'

'Yes, it is. Don't lie to me. I hate it when people lie.'

Dean took a deep breath. Maybe it was time to see if Lucien knew what he was talking about, or if Dean was about to make a massive error of judgement.

'Okay. The truth is I'm missing my son's birthday party.'

Lydia's face fell. 'Why on earth are you still here? Go!'

Dean shook his head. 'This is my job, and I take that seriously. I am choosing to be here because I care about you, and you deserve to have someone with you just as much as my son does.

And, as it happens, my son is with someone who does care about him right now.'

'The person you've been texting?'

'Yes. There's no one I'd be happier leaving my son with than him. My son is fine. He's happy and safe. My job today is to keep *you* happy and safe. Is that okay with you?'

She nodded.

'Now, do you want to watch a video of my son smearing chocolate cake all over Dr Benedict?'

'Yes, please!'

She laughed and bounded over to Dean's side.

After a minute, she nudged his arm. 'Sorry about the knife thing. I never really had one.'

'It's okay.'

Two hours later Lydia was collected by the crisis team. While Dean had waited, he'd managed to get Lydia into CBT sessions starting in a fortnight, and had found a support group she could go to locally, with other young people with experience of mental illness.

Dean grabbed his phone to text Lucien the good news that he was one step closer to getting home, but found his phone was finally dead.

He'd give himself a reasonable nine and a half out of ten for being a doctor today. Now he just had to pull up his score for being a dad. And after missing his son's entire birthday party he was not off to the best start.

Dean took a deep breath, pushed open the hospital door, and stepped out into the night. Only for a nurse to rush directly towards him from the car park and grab his arm.

'Are you Dr Vasquez?'

Dean nodded.

'You're needed in the family room.'

CHAPTER NINE

LUCIEN HAD BEEN so careful, trying to do everything right. After he'd put Rafael to bed he'd done some tidying, cleared up all the major messes, and made sure to put all the leftovers in the fridge. He'd manoeuvred the cake into a large Tupperware box which had only just managed to contain it. Then he'd looked at the remaining mess and realised it wasn't happening. He would clear it up in the morning.

The sofa looked plush and warm, and he decided to lie down, watch some TV and wait for Dean to get home. He'd want a full report on the party when he got back, and Lucien was bubbling over with excitement to tell him how well it had gone.

But in the end Lucien's emotional and physical exhaustion and the softness of the sofa won out, and after the cat joined him, purring softly, it was over.

Lucien fell asleep not half an hour after he sat down.

He woke suddenly, convinced he'd heard a noise, but not sure what it might have been. The room was dark, and almost silent but for the TV still quietly playing. He sat up and saw that it was still only ten o clock. Maybe Dean was back? But he couldn't hear anyone moving around, and Dean was never this quiet.

He tipped the cat off his lap on to the sofa and checked the kitchen, before setting off up the stairs and looking in Dean's room. Nothing. He explored the bathroom, and his own room, before peeking around Rafael's door.

He wasn't in his bed.

Lucien's heart dropped. But surely he was just in the other bathroom. Or maybe Lucien had missed seeing him in the kitchen—he was very small, after all.

Lucien checked every single room again, more carefully this time, calling Rafael's name.

'Rafael? Where are you, buddy?'

Dean had never mentioned anything like sleep-walking, or told him that Rafael had a propensity for wandering around at night. But finally he'd checked every room, and every wardrobe, and he was starting to panic.

He stood in the hall. All the coats were still on their pegs, but Rafael's shoes were missing. He was sure he'd tidied them away just hours before…

Damn it.

Lucien yanked open the door and flew outside, yelling Rafael's name into the freezing cold night. There was no one at the front, but when Lucien ran around the side of the house to the patio he was confronted with the worst thing he'd ever seen in his life.

Lucien stood alone in the hospital's family room, terrified and completely at a loss as to what to do. He fumbled his phone from his pocket and nearly dropped it on the floor before trying to get hold of Dean again.

Nothing.

How had Rafael even got out of the house in the middle of the night? Let alone managed to fall out of the damn oak tree?

All the guilt and fear he'd felt after his mother's death returned and hit Lucien like a truck, and he sat down before his knees gave way. Regardless of the how and why, Rafael was badly hurt—and it was all Lucien's fault. Yet again, someone Lucien loved had come to harm on his watch.

Lucien rocked slightly, staring unseeing at the pattern on the linoleum floor, trying to figure out what on earth he'd missed. How could he have done things differently to avoid this? Maybe he couldn't have. If people got close to him, they got hurt. He couldn't believe he'd been so reckless as to let himself forget that.

He couldn't get the image he'd seen out of his

head… Rafael lying on the patio under the tree… his blood mixing with the fallen leaves…

Lucien sent another worried message to Dean.

A sudden thought struck him. What if Dean got home before he saw his messages and went outside? He'd see the blood covering the patio. There was so much blood…

He knew he had to think straight—had to ask the staff if Dean was still in the hospital. Or perhaps it would be quicker to run and look for Dean himself. But then Lucien wouldn't be here if Rafael needed him.

Dean would want him to look after Rafael first.

He had to stay put.

The door to the family room slammed open and Dean rushed in, looking sick with worry, his eyes wild.

'Dean!'

'The nurse told me you were here. What the hell is happening? Where's Rafael?'

Lucien, seeing that Dean was terrified, lost his own fear immediately and went into caretaker mode. He spoke calmly and reached for Dean's shoulder. 'The doctors are in with him now. I'm waiting to hear.'

'What do you mean? Waiting to hear what? Why aren't you in there? How could you leave him alone?'

'I wasn't allowed in, Dean,' Lucien said firmly. 'You know that.'

'I don't care. What the hell has happened to my boy?'

Lucien felt guilt surge up again.

He manoeuvred Dean over to the chairs at the edge of the room and gently pushed him down on to the nearest one. 'Sit down, and I'll explain what happened.'

Dean sat, surprising Lucien by not fighting him every step of the way. Dean was paler than he'd ever seen him.

'It was after the party…everyone had gone home. I put Rafael to bed, and everything was fine. I tried to wait up for you, but I must have fallen asleep on the sofa. Then I woke up. I'd heard a noise—which I guess must have been him going outside. But I didn't know that then. I thought you'd come home, so I looked for you first. Then I checked on Rafael, and that's when I noticed he was gone. I'm sorry… I should have checked on him first.'

Dean shook his head desperately. 'Get to the point. What happened?'

'He went out while I was asleep. The piñata… it was still outside. I'd hung it from the oak tree. He'd said earlier he wanted to check inside, to see if there were any sweets left, and I told him we'd look tomorrow. I guess he couldn't wait… I had no idea, Dean. I should have taken it down myself, but I didn't think he'd climb the tree.'

'He climbed the tree?'

'Yes. I hung the piñata quite high. He fell a long way, Dean. On to the patio. He must have landed on one hand. He's broken his arm badly, banged his head… And he could have been lying there for up to ten minutes before I found him…'

'He was lying alone…unconscious…outside in the freezing cold, because you didn't think to check on my son straight away when you heard a noise in the middle of the night?'

Lucien swallowed and nodded.

A doctor burst in. Lucien recognised her as someone he'd known professionally for years, and knew she happened to be the most experienced paediatric surgeon in the hospital.

His stress levels dropped infinitesimally.

'This is Dean—Rafael's father.' Lucien introduced the two quickly.

Dean shot up. They shared a perfunctory handshake and she gestured for him to take a seat. Dean sat immediately, and the doctor got right to the point.

'We'll need to set his arm. His ulna is broken. It's a clean break, but it pierced the skin and he's lost some blood. He'll need to be given a general anaesthetic before we take him to Theatre.'

The doctor's bleeper went off and she excused herself.

'I'll be back in just a moment to take you to him.'

Lucien felt sick.

'I'm so sorry, Dean. I just wish you'd been with Rafael instead of me.'

'Are you saying this is *my* fault?'

'No, of course not! I'm saying the complete opposite.'

'Because maybe if you had been a better doctor to Lydia then none of this would have happened. You didn't even want me to be here with her tonight. What? Am I not good enough?'

'No, that wasn't about *you*.' Lucien desperately tried to explain. 'When I was Rafael's age my mother used to put her patients ahead of me all the time. I didn't want to see you doing the same thing to Rafael.'

Lucien knew that had come out wrong as soon as he said it.

'You think you can do a better job?'

'No, I'm not saying that.'

'You think you're a better father to Rafael than me? Because, from where I'm standing, missing the first six years of his life and then letting him fall out of a damn tree isn't a great start.'

'What are you talking about? How could I...?'

'Just—please, shut up, Lucien. I can't do this. I can't do it any more.'

'Do what?' Lucien was bewildered.

'Use your big brain for once and work it out. Why do you think I turned up here out of nowhere?'

Lucien stepped back. 'I don't know why...'

'To find his biological father. To find *you*.'

Dean's words seemed to echo off the walls and the shiny linoleum floor of the corridor.

Lucien felt disorientated, and all he could see was Dean's angry green gaze.

'How can he possibly be mine? I've only been with one woman in my entire life, and she didn't have a child. Charlie's a doctor somewhere… miles away. Rafael's mother is—'

'Rafael's mother is Charlie. Charlotte died, Lucien. She's dead.'

Lucien backed away further.

He saw Dean's fury finally soften, and he reached out towards him. But it was too late. Lucien couldn't bear the thought of Dean touching him. And wasn't that a kick to the heart?

'Wait!' said Dean, his voice breaking on the word. 'Look, I was going to tell you today…after Rafael's party. I just didn't want to ruin it.'

'Well, you've done a pretty decent job of that anyway.' Lucien paused as he realised something. 'Is that why you spent the whole night here? To avoid having to tell me the truth?'

'No!'

Dean looked absolutely heartbroken. But Lucien shook his head. If he believed what Dean was saying now, then Dean had been lying to him since the second they'd met.

Was any of it real? Or was their whole relationship a lie? What possible reason could Dean have to do this to him?

Overwhelmed, Lucien knew he needed to get away. He was desperate for air…and most of all desperate to be away from Dean.

And just like that, Lucien left.

Dean's worst fear had come true. He'd been abandoned—again. By the one person he'd hoped would never leave.

Part of Dean already regretted everything he'd said to Lucien. But there was no way he could leave Rafael and follow him—and in any case he was still too terrified and angry to speak lucidly.

The doctor returned.

'Please take me to my son,' Dean managed to force out.

The doctor nodded and led him quickly down a corridor.

Dean knew it was unreasonable to be so angry. Lucien wasn't really at fault for any of this. But Dean had so much pent-up fear inside him it had to come out in some direction.

He'd hoped to feel some sort of relief when the truth of Lucien's identity finally came out, but no part of him could feel relief or even process what had happened while Rafael was lying in a hospital bed.

Rafael was in a private room. His eyes were

red-rimmed, but he was awake, and he started crying quietly when Dean rushed to his side.

'Oh, baby, I'm so sorry I wasn't here. I came as fast as I could.'

Dean ran his hands quickly over his son's face and uninjured arm, then kissed his head.

Rafael sniffled.

'How's your arm feel, sweetheart?'

'They're going to give me a blue cast.'

Rafael's voice was so weak it broke Dean's heart, but he smiled widely for Rafael.

'It'll look amazing.'

A chair appeared from somewhere behind him, and Dean accepted the seat without taking his eyes off Rafael. He stroked Rafael's hair with one hand and held his tiny warm hand with the other. Rafael had been given some painkillers, but they had to wait for a slot in Theatre.

Once Rafael's gaze was firmly on the action film playing on the screen in the corner of the room, Dean allowed himself to quietly break down…just for a moment. Silent tears ran down his cheeks and he subtly wiped them away with his sleeve.

Rafael coughed, and Dean grabbed his son's hand, holding it firmly.

He couldn't help but feel an empty space next to them both, where Lucien should be.

CHAPTER TEN

LUCIEN HAD ONLY spent a minute outside, breathing deeply as Dean had taught him at the auction, before he'd calmed down enough to walk away from the hospital. All he wanted to do was rush back inside and be with Rafael, but he couldn't bear to see Dean.

He was angry. With Dean, but even more so with himself.

He got a taxi home as quickly as possible, and the first thing he did was grab the garden hose and clean the bloodstained patio. Over his career he'd seen his fair share of blood and bodily fluids, but washing Rafael's blood off the flagstones into the roses made him so nauseous he had to lean against the cold brick wall for a minute to collect himself.

After that, he knew he just needed to be alone. Alone somewhere that wasn't inside a house surrounded by Dean's belongings, his smell, and memories of every tainted moment Lucien had spent falling for him.

Not to mention every moment Dean could have told him the truth and had chosen not to.

After striding mindlessly through the cold on autopilot, he found himself outside the tumbledown church. He gazed up at the crooked tower, his breath clouding above him.

This was how it felt to be betrayed.

He'd avoided close relationships for so long—by accident or by choice he wasn't sure. But he'd managed to steer clear of all the heartbreak and emotional complications he'd seen his colleagues deal with so often. He'd almost let himself feel he was above all that silly emotional nonsense. He was too cerebral…too ruled by intellect.

More fool him.

He shoved open the church door, only to find it was no warmer inside. He pulled his coat more tightly around him. There were so many thoughts rolling around in his head it was impossible to focus on one, so they swirled inside him like a murmuration of starlings, fighting one another for attention.

His heart raced as he relived Dean's words at the hospital. His hands curled into tight fists, and he wished there was something he could throw across the room, just to see it shatter. But he was hardly going to throw a stack of dusty bibles, or a rusting sacramental chalice, and a wooden pew might be a bit optimistic even accounting for rage-induced strength.

Anyway, that wasn't him.

He let out a huge, shuddering breath and felt the anger leave him. And found he was only left with pain.

Dean had lied to him. Lucien had a son—a perfect, beautiful son—and he'd missed out on years of knowing him.

Rafael was his.

Rafael was hurt.

Rafael was hurt and it was Lucien's fault.

He'd done it again. He'd let someone get close, and his own stupid mistakes had almost got someone he loved killed. He was better off alone, and Dean and Rafael were certainly better off without him.

Lucien couldn't face climbing the steps to the tower so he sank down on to a pew instead. Leaning forward with his head in his hands, he cursed his traitorous heart. He couldn't bear the thought of seeing Dean, but Dean was the only person he desperately wished were with him. Dean with his strong hands, his calm voice, his beautiful green eyes that burned deep into his soul.

Ugh.

Lucien sat in the cold church for hours, until his backside was numb and he had trouble feeling his fingers and toes. He figured he wasn't the first person who'd tried to repent of his sins with some good old-fashioned penance within these four walls.

There were still dozens of abandoned candles at the front of the church. Dust-covered votive candles that had never been lit in memory of anyone—at least not for a couple of decades.

Lucien finally felt the urge to get up, and he rubbed his hands together to get some feeling back. He strode up the aisle, closed his eyes and blew the dust from the candles, then fished around in his pocket for his lighter and picked one up. Once it flickered into life, he stared at the tiny strong flame until the shape burned itself into his retinas, then he leaned on the votive stand with both hands, bowed his head and prayed.

He might not have prayed in years, and he didn't even know what he did or didn't believe in, but now he prayed—to God or Mother Nature, to luck or fate, to anyone who was listening—that Rafael and Dean would forgive him. He prayed so hard that his fingers hurt from grabbing on to the stand so tightly.

After a minute, he breathed deeply in and out, focused again on the shape of the flame that he could still see in front of his closed eyes, and felt a strange sense of calm overcome him. He was still scared, and he was still confused, but he knew where he needed to be.

Being alone had always used to be the cure for anything, but that just wasn't going to cut it any more.

Why was he even angry in the first place? The

most perfect family in the world was right there, waiting for him. He realised now that had always been true—even before Dean had let slip his biological connection to Rafael. And maybe he could be part of that family—maybe he could have it all.

He would always feel responsible for what had happened to Rafael. But it wasn't about him, or his guilt—he was irrelevant. The only thing that mattered was Rafael being okay. And Dean. He needed Dean to be okay too. And right now Lucien was in completely the wrong place. He needed to go to them and do whatever was necessary to make that happen.

Lucien didn't know what Dean would say when he found him. He didn't know if Dean would be able to forgive him. But when Lucien put all his confusion and fear aside he knew he had to be brave and take a risk if Dean still wanted him. And Dean might have concealed the truth about Rafael, but when Lucien looked inside himself he knew Dean hadn't lied about his feelings.

Lucien smiled down at the dancing flame. As always, this place had done its job and helped him see everything more clearly.

He couldn't imagine his life without either Dean or Rafael.

The birthday party might have proved to him that kids could be a nightmare, but he loved a particular one. Getting to know both Dean and Rafael had made him an infinitely better person, more comfortable being his true self than he'd ever been before. And Rafael being his was the best thing that had ever happened to him. He could have everything he wanted if he was just brave enough to take it.

A few hours later Rafael had been given a general anaesthetic, had had an X-ray taken, his broken bones put in alignment and his arm set. Now he sat up in bed, brand-new blue cast in place, still watching the television. Totally casual…as if they hadn't all just been through the most stressful day of their lives.

A nurse's aide came in with a small pot of red jelly, a spoon and a new cup of water. As the aide left, Helen knocked on the glass door and waved at Dean from the corridor.

Dean jumped up and squeezed Rafael's shoulder. 'Don't eat that yet. I'll be back in a second.'

Dean joined Helen in the corridor, but left the door open in case Rafael needed him.

'What are you doing here? It's the middle of the night.'

'It's daylight, Dean. It's five a.m. And there are no secrets in Little Champney. I got a call first thing, telling me what had happened, and I drove right over. How is he?'

Dean blinked at the nearest window. She was right—the light outside was getting brighter.

'He has a broken arm, but I think I can take

him home today or tomorrow. He just needs to sleep.'

'And how are you? You must have been through the wringer.'

'Me? God, I'm fine. Forget about me.'

Helen gave him a disapproving look. 'You're no good to him exhausted. You look bloody awful.'

'Ouch, don't spare my feelings or anything.'

Helen ignored him, stepped quietly into the room, and grabbed Rafael's notes from the foot of the bed.

'You should sleep,' she said, leafing through the notes. 'I'll sit with Rafael. Oh, and you should check on Lucien too. Apparently he didn't look so hot when he left last night.'

'I'll do that,' he murmured in reply.

Helen rubbed Dean's arm. 'I'll be back in ten minutes. Give the poor kid his jelly.'

Back by Rafael's side, Dean spooned up some jelly and offered it up to his son's mouth.

'I can feed myself,' said Rafael, his voice croaky, but stronger than it had been a few hours ago.

'That's funny, because I'm pretty sure I remember Helen's kids feeding you sweets all evening at the auction.'

'S'not the same.'

'I know.' Dean rubbed the back of Rafael's hand softly. 'But just this once let me do it. You need to rest as much as possible.'

Rafael rolled his eyes like a teenager, but let Dean continue.

Dean had completely missed out on feeding Rafael like this, so he was going to make the most of it while he could.

Rafael accepted a few spoonsful and then waved the spoon away. 'Where's Lucien?' he asked.

Dean blinked. 'Well, he's giving us some space…' Dean ate a spoonful of Rafael's jelly himself. 'You know he saved your life today?'

'He did?' Rafael stared up at Dean, wide-eyed.

'Yes. First off he found you outside, in time to stop you freezing to death.' Dean adjusted the blanket over Rafael. 'By the way, we're due a serious talk about how leaving the house at night alone is *not* okay, and how climbing a tree in the dead of night is extremely unwise.'

Rafael nodded sheepishly, and Dean squeezed his arm and kissed his hand.

'And then he got you to hospital and made sure you were safe and looked after.'

'Is he angry with me?'

'Who? Lucien? No, of course not.'

'He said I had to wait until the morning to check the piñata.'

'Yeah, he told me. Why didn't you?'

Rafael didn't answer.

'Can I take a guess?'

Rafael nodded.

'I think, maybe, you were cross about me missing your party. Which is totally understandable. And that made you act up a little bit.'

Rafael scratched his nose and stared at his jelly. 'Maybe.'

'I'm so sorry I missed it, Raf. And I'm so sorry you're spending your birthday in hospital. We can have another party when you get out of here. And it'll be ten times better than the one I missed.'

'The one you missed was really good.'

'It was?' Dean smiled. 'I'm glad. That means I'll have to work even harder to make the next one ten times better, won't I?'

The doctor swept in with a nurse, who checked Rafael's temperature, pulse, and blood pressure.

'Okay, Rafael, you're doing wonderfully,' said the doctor with a smile. 'At the moment what he needs is sleep, Dr Vasquez. So now would be a good time for you to go home, shower, rest…then get some of your son's things and come back in a few hours.'

Dean could recognise a doctor telling a parent politely to get lost. He'd done it himself plenty of times. But now it was his turn to completely ignore a professional.

'There's no way I'm sleeping, or leaving his side for long. But I will run home and grab some stuff.'

Ten minutes later Rafael was asleep. Dean stroked his hair softly for a little while longer, not wanting to leave him. This had truly been a wake-up call for realising how much he loved his son. The ferocity of his love for Rafael scared him a little bit. But now that he knew his son was stable, and not in any immediate danger, there was something he needed to do.

Dean found Helen waiting patiently out in the corridor. She promised not to leave Rafael's bedside for a second. And once she'd sworn that she would call him immediately if anything happened whatsoever, Dean gave her a long hug and left the hospital.

Dean unlocked the front door of the house. He could feel that Lucien wasn't there as soon as he entered the hall. The house was too quiet, too cold.

'Lucien?' he shouted anyway, just in case.

But there was no answer. He jogged up the stairs, checking inside all the rooms on the way up to his bedroom.

Nothing.

Why had he kept his secret for so long? Dean asked himself. Towards the end he knew he'd been lying for his own sake, not Rafael's. He'd been terrified that Lucien would leave, and now his worst nightmares had come true. He'd been abandoned again, by the one person he'd hoped would never go.

He wanted to crawl into his bed, hide away and lick his wounds, as he always did.

Dean sank on to the bed and plugged in his phone charger. He checked his notifications and finally saw all the increasingly desperate texts Lucien had sent him.

They were hard to read, but somehow they made him fall in love with Lucien all over again.

Dean, please, I don't want you to panic, but Raf's had an accident. I'm at the hospital with him now. Find me as soon as you see this. Obviously. What else would you do? He's going to be okay, so please don't be scared.

I'm so sorry. It's all my fault.

Not that it's about me.

But I am sorry.

I guess your phone must be out of power. Or out of signal.

Damn, you're going to be so scared when you get home and find the place empty.

Maybe I can get Helen to be there to meet you. But she's not picking up either. Damn it.

I'm so sorry.

There's still no news, by the way. I'm just sorry in general. Not because I was about to tell you bad news.

I'm making this worse with every text, aren't I?

Just get here, please. I'm in the family room.

I miss you.

Anyone who could make him smile while reading a live commentary of the worst night of his life was someone he could not let go.

As Dean sat alone in the empty house, he let the night's trauma and all his doubts slip away. He only remembered what Lucien meant to him—to them both. There was no denying it. If Dean still needed proof that Lucien was everything he could wish for in a father for Rafael, then this was it. And while they were at it he might just be everything Dean could wish for in a person to spend his life with.

Not that he needed proof. He'd known it for a long time. Rafael needed both his dads.

Dean felt a rush of courage. He would fight for what he loved. And Dean knew exactly where Lucien would be.

He left through the back door and rushed to

the garden. He came to an abrupt stop on the patio, nearly walking straight into the piñata. His heart skipped as he saw the place where Rafael must have fallen. Where the patio was clean. He knew Rafael had lost blood there, and his mind projected it so that he could almost see it there, below him, but there was nothing.

Lucien must have come home after their argument and cleaned it up so Dean didn't have to see it. Strange, the things that could seem romantic.

He messaged Lucien only four words as he hurried down to the end of the road towards the woods.

I'm on my way.

Seconds later, Dean's phone chimed with a video call request. Dean answered immediately, and smiled when he saw Lucien's bewildered, open face. So different from the last time he'd seen him on camera, on the first day they'd ever met.

'You don't know where I am,' said Lucien.

'Of course I do.'

And as Dean saw the flickering candlelight behind Lucien's head he knew he was right.

'How are you video calling me? You hate doing this,' Dean panted as he hurried through the field and slipped across the bridge outside the church.

'I needed to see your face.'

Dean smiled. 'More fool you. Apparently I look awful.'

'No, you don't. How is he?' Lucien asked, looking stricken.

Dean couldn't bear it that he wasn't with Lucien yet, so he could soothe that look away.

'Raf's going to be fine. Everything went perfectly. Don't worry. I'm almost with you.'

As Dean ended the call Lucien appeared at the church door.

Dean ran through the church yard, dodging past the gravestones, and launched himself into Lucien's strong arms.

The second Lucien held him, all the emotions Dean had been holding in for hours streamed out, and soon Lucien's shoulder was damp.

Lucien squeezed Dean tight to his chest, rubbing his back slowly with one hand. 'I'm so sorry,' Lucien whispered into Dean's neck. 'Is he really okay?'

'Yes!' Dean sniffed and cleared his throat. 'The procedure went well and they've set his arm. He's out of the woods.' Dean felt Lucien relax in his arms. 'Thanks to you,' Dean added.

'To me? It's my fault he's in there.'

'How? Did you push him out of a tree?'

'No. But—'

'But nothing.'

Dean pulled back and held Lucien's shoulders

firmly, to get a good look at him. 'How are you feeling?'

Lucien smiled fondly at him. 'I'm fine, Dean. I promise.'

Dean drew back. 'Lucien, I have some things I need to say to you.'

Lucien looked worried.

'I have a lot of apologies to make. So bed in.'

Dean sat down on the nearest pew and took Lucien's hand, pulling him down next to him.

'First of all, I'm sorry I shouted at you in the hospital earlier. I was scared, and I got defensive and lashed out. You didn't deserve that.'

Lucien shrugged as if it was no big deal.

'And secondly, I'm sorry I've been lying to you all this time.'

Lucien's gaze dropped, and it was obvious how much that had hurt him. Suddenly Dean was scared to keep going, but he knew he had to get everything out in the open.

'And finally, I'm so sorry I told you about Rafael and Charlie in the way that I did. I never planned for things to come out like that. You'd just found out you have a son, and then you found out Charlie had died too.'

'That was a shock,' Lucien admitted. 'But I would have already known if I'd kept in touch with anyone. It's strange, really…she and I weren't all that close, but I've never known someone so full of life. I can't believe she's gone. Poor Rafael.'

'It's been hard for him. But he's brave.'

'He really is.'

'And I'm sorry your mother made you feel second best,' said Dean. 'You're right—I would never want to make Rafael feel that way. But we can learn from the past and do things differently.'

'How?'

'We have each other. If I have to put a patient first for one night, then Rafael has you. And vice versa. He's so lucky he has both of us to love him. He won't ever get the chance to feel second best to anything.'

Lucien's eyes filled with emotion, and Dean let Lucien pull him even closer, luxuriating in the warmth of his body wrapped around him.

'I hated lying to you,' Dean said. 'If it's all right with you, I never want to do it again.'

'I would be okay with that.'

Lucien rested his head against Dean's shoulder and found Dean's hand with his.

'So you knew who I was when you applied for the job?'

'Yes. You're the reason we came here. I wanted Rafael to have you in his life, but I didn't know you. I couldn't risk that you would hurt him or leave him. I had to make sure you were safe. I never expected that you would be perfect, or that I would fall in love with you.'

Lucien's fingers tightened on Dean's and they kissed deeply. Lucien stroked Dean's hair, then let his hand linger on Dean's cheek. Dean's eyes watered at the gentle touch, but he blinked his tears away.

'When did you decide that I was safe for Rafael?' asked Lucien.

'Pretty quickly. Then I had to figure out if you were safe for me. I started to get scared that I'd be the one who got hurt or left behind. I'd been keeping the truth hidden for so long... This huge, life-destroying secret. How could you ever forgive me for that?'

'Not life-destroying. Life-saving. And of course I forgive you. I love you too, Dean. I've never loved anyone before—I don't think I even wanted to. Or maybe I just thought nobody could love me back.'

'Well, now you know.'

They kissed again. Then Dean kicked gently at the pew ahead of him and kept his gaze off Lucien.

'How do you feel about Rafael?'

Lucien turned Dean's face gently back towards him. 'I love him, Dean. I've loved him for a long time. Maybe even longer than I've loved you.'

Dean's smile grew, his eyes wet. 'He's pretty lovable, huh?'

'Just like his dad.' Lucien winked.

Dean laughed. Lucien was terrible at winking. It was more of a blink. But it was probably the most adorable thing he'd ever seen.

'I don't know if you mean me or you,' said Dean.

Lucien shrugged, smiling playfully, and then his face dropped. 'Jesus Christ… I'm a dad.'

'Yeah, congratulations. It's a boy.'

Dean held out his hand, and Lucien took it with no hesitation. 'Are you ready to hole up in a hospital room with me and figure out how to explain to a seven-year-old what a biological father is?'

'I can't think of anything else I'd rather do.'

And as he walked out across the mossy graveyard, in the shadow of the crooked spire, with Lucien's warm hand grasped in his own, Dean felt as if he was home for the first time in his life.

* * * * *